The Story Of MrSir

(WORD FOR THE RECORD)

Presented by

MPHO MATLHABEGOANE

Copyright and Publishing

For orders and reviews, you may reach us on:
mrsirmatlhabegoane@gmail.com
SMS or Call: 0720482700/ 0627962563
WhatsApp: 0720482700
Facebook: MrSir Placidfray
Instagram: @MrSir_placidfray
Twitter: @tso_MrSir
YouTube: MrSir Placidfray

This book is pure fiction. Names and characters in this book are fictitious.

Contents

Foreword

"I never let the sun sets on a disagreement with anybody who means a lot to me."-Thomas John Watson Sr., Founder of IBM.

I am so honored to be offered an opportunity to contribute to a book such as this and I send my sincere gratitude to the author for offering me this auspicious window. I am so thrilled by the wisdom imparted in this book and confident that whoever bestows their hands on this book will surely obsess over it.

The Story Of MrSir (Word For The Record) is about a man who encountered many challenges in his life and highlighted some milestones in his success with the help of being exposed to a psychologist. Its focal storyline is constructed with reminiscences of MrSir's past life events (sad, funny, romantic, critical, motivational, educational, nail biting, etc) which all connect to one thing: Mind Control attack. MrSir is a poet – hence there are poems in the story. He is a facilitator – hence there are educational highlights attached to *'Word For The Record'* digressions.

This book is meant to appreciate psychologists for the 4IR era that we are heading to. Most Africans do not believe in the concept of psychology. Mental health to them has to do with witchcraft, and neither biological nor environmental factors. What are genetics to typical Africans? They are western things! That's what we believe. This book covers several aspects of MrSir's life where the psychologist intervened and was able to help him to return to his state of equilibrium so that he may be able to face the daily hassles of life.

The author is trying to educate us about the importance and effectiveness of psychologists because he realized that our generation is going through a lot of pressure of change and keeping up, which in turn lead to depression due to keeping things to ourselves, bulking them up and the sundry - so the idea of the whole book is psychology being a solution in a world of art, science, technology and mathematics. The author mentioned that religion helps, but without psychologically finding our grounds religion becomes unclear.

Many of us grew up not knowing that there is such thing as a psychologist and some in their 20s, I reckon, even yet, are not aware of this discipline. Africans need to be educated and be encouraged to consult with psychologists and counselors when walking through this journey of life for the better functionality in all functional areas. South Africa needs more psychologists and counselors in all hospitals and clinics - public or private. A life without psychology is meaningless!

It is crucial for individuals to seek help when struggling with containing some aspects of their lives. Recently the author and I hosted an online hackathon (Seminar) on the topic 'Depression is real' and many individuals mentioned how hard it is to deal with it since our society is not well oriented on mental illness. It is demoralizing that they have no social support. In our society people with mental illnesses are dismissed, neglected and judged, and this could be because of not being aware of how serious it is and how it negatively affects one's daily life. The main conclusion was to seek professional help since our social support is failing us in helping with walking through this disorder and to be mindful of whom we share depressive episodes with to avoid being surmised.

As I wind up, I want to urge you to read this story with its purpose in your mind, and note that psychology is a discipline that the society should be well versed on and should be well oriented about. Psychologists and counselors are available at hospitals and some clinics to assist us on whatever we are going through - small or big. Let us come together and fight the stigma of mental illnesses in our societies and encourage one another to get professional help.

There is some romance in this story - well it is almost mostly based on it. Even if it is a fictitious adventure, suspense, comedy and the sundry, we might still wonder through the pages and be astonished. However, the predominant message of the author is that the main character got through it all by having a session with a lady who is a psychologist. In its context, flow, content and lessons, it is quite evident that the hope of the author is that this book will remind us of the resources we have, that we should utilize them, and think out of the box when dealing with life's problems. He wishes that this book will start a conversation, a debate and even a controversy, but at the end let us all support each other emotionally. Young or old, we all need counseling in our lives. Go ahead and get yours!

-Katlego Seshoka

Chapter A - Alpha signs of the mystery.

It was 3 A.M when I missed her first call. I picked up the phone on her third attempt, and before I could even say a word, she said, "MrSir! MrSir! Whatever he says, please say no word to him! Please! He's gonna be on your door as soon as the sun rises. Just ignore him. Please!"

She sounded as though her tears had just evaporated from a shriek.

Who would yawn and stretch so as to startle from a sleep when they received such calls to do better? By the moment I responded, my mind had already faded from a thought of ´I was sleeping.´ Then I threw a mixture of interjections and haphazardly asked, "Wait-wait! Who are 'he'? Who is 'you'? Goddamn! What you talking 'bout?"

Did she reply? Did she even bother answering my questions? Guess what - she hung up on me! Yes, before I knew it, there was already a Tuu-sound hitting my tympanum. Luckily, it wasn't a private number, so I tried calling her back and all I got was, "You have less than three Rands and -" then I disconnected quickly, trying to deny it a chance to *chow* my remaining cents because I thought it was voicemail.

I tried again and that time it was, "Welcome to the mailbox of-" then it went mute. I had a feeling of awe, I was freaked out and I wasn't thinking straight, so I tried again. Before I knew it, the machine tuned to, "You have reached your call limit, please recharge your..."

I then passed the time by counting the troughs on the imaginary corrugated iron of the illusionary roof. Had I not kept my mind busy, relativity would have made the clock look dormant. It started getting brighter and brighter, and Tada! The sun appeared...

Word For The Record: The sun didn't necessarily rise. The earth simply continued its rotation around the sun until our eyes reached the light emitted. The sun does not move!

I expected a knock from the mysterious ´he´, or at least a call from the security guy downstairs. A part of me was fretting and another was curious. I wondered if we stayed in the same building or city, and whether I knew him or he knew me. I eventually pictured an obese bloke claiming that I had stolen his girlfriend - and - well - the image was rather intimidating than funny for my sense of humor.

I switched my hallucinations to a skinny chap, with nerds and a squeaky voice, trying to - Oops!

Tring - Tring! Tring - Tring!

My imaginations were interrupted by an anticipated call from the security guy downstairs. It was a ´you have a visitor with neither an ID Book nor a student card´ call. I was unfamiliar with his name, so I just trotted to the elevator. The space in it allowed me to wonder and worry until I reached the ground floor. I'd say that I crossed my fingers if I was a coconut (a person who possesses a black race with qualities of a white man - brown on the outside, but white in the inside. Get it?), instead I hoped for the better and said my prayers in my heart.

As the elevator's doors repelled, my sight reached an empty reception. Both the security guy and the mysterious dude were beyond my visual reach. My conscience warned me against going out of the building, but I dared to. Immediately when my forehead pinned the ´out of the building´ territory, my whole body felt an instantaneous loss of heat.

Word For The Record: You don't catch cold, you lose heat. Cold is the absence of heat, not the opposite of it. Therefore, cold neither exists nor can it be transferred. Stop substantiating concepts that modify the absence of the existing ones! Another example is: Light and darkness.

For an African, that feeling of 'catching cold' could only mean a presence of a ghost. In my thoughts, I fed my ego by telling myself that he probably took to his heels when he realized that I would have defeated him. The ego got well-fed and fat that I ended up shouting, "Are you gonna hide like a napkin-wearing baby? Huh? Be a man, dammit!"

(You know that's what we all do when we are frightened. We always tend to pass our fears onto our opponents.)

Before I could yell more, the security guy asked if I'm talking to anyone in sight. I answered with "maybe" when the thought of "Where the hell had he been and when did he get here?" knocked on my cranium. I opened the cranium for that question and welcomed it by asking him. In response, he said, "What do you mean? You passed me right here, Sir!" I couldn't trust my retention at that point of time.

Maybe I started chewing trees with my teeth (*ke jele ditlhare ka meno*). Okay - wait - that phrase could only make sense if it wasn't said in English. It's a Tswana (South African Language) idiomatic expression for when one had gone literally mad.

I glanced at my timepiece and realized that I was running late for my first and only class of the day (which was my last for the semester due to exams). "Mr. Security, I'm pretty rushed off my feet now. I believe you have something to tell me when I return, right?" As I approached the elevator, I announced every syllable, making sure I was sane and wide awake.

A second after finishing that phrase, I saw the need to use the stairs and my legs automatically hoisted me up them. I almost tripped on the first step. I checked if no one was looking before I sped up to my door.

(We all check if someone is looking when we trip, be it on stairs or anywhere else, don't we? It's even funny when we assume that people didn't notice, while they were simply trying hard not to show us that they actually saw us.)

In a hurry or not, I was always aware of how I left things. I could precisely tell when they had changed. Well - as soon as I arrived at my door, I noticed something peculiar. I had left my door ajar, but I found it fully closed. Surely that evoked my observations. There were two possibilities; one was that my room had been cleared by thieves, and another was that it was occupied by a serial - somebody.

I needed to take a quick shower, and since my toiletry bag was inside I had no choice but to just budge in like a callous brave tenant. Just as my instincts had anticipated, I found my closet as empty as it was, when I first moved in.

"Woah! Them what? Sneakers too? NAH NAH NAH! This ain't happening! Nat today! Nat to Meee! Naaah!" I shouted. I then called out names of my flat-mates, particularly those whose names my tongue felt fit enough to pronounce off the cuff.

"Tiblo! Toni! Coco! Mash - o - Dick!" I almost swallowed my tongue when I attempted the last one. I admit that I may have had a tongue twisting last name, but the bloke's names were alien to my home language. Both Mash and Dick were his real names. (He's so going to nail me for writing that.) An eerie thing was that we hardly used his nickname. That's if he had a nick name. Otherwise, they were my family at 'home away from home', so we said...

In a nick of time, they were in my room and the first thing Tiblo said was, "Is it spring already? Yah neh, course can chow that bad, can't it?" I chuckled a little, calming my hackles. Before I could remark, Toni commented, "This is more like theft than spring - cleaning dawg! Can't you be less stupid?" Sarcasm was our only language, and the good thing about us was that we never took anything personal - we just loved attacking each other. I reckon we enjoyed the pleasure of our reactions than of our attacks. It was crazy!

Tiblo had to reply. Well - he did and he said, "Literal minds! Don't you have a song to compose?" Toni and Tiblo were both musicians. Tiblo was an EDM Producer, but he was studying Marketing and Communication Skills. Toni was both an RnB singer and a pianist, but he was studying Sound Engineering. In a way, I noted the contradiction in Tiblo's reply, but my condition didn't allow me to comment.

Before Piet could attempt to respond, Ammo (who was also both a pianist and an RnB Singer, Hip Hop Producer and studying Sound Engineering) intruded, but he was calmer than all of them on that day, "Dawg, whadup? What actually went down here?"

My chest suddenly felt light, and my mood lighter. My jaws felt heavy, and my tongue longer. My mouth secreted an abnormal quantity of saliva and my throat swelled. To my past experiences and the prevailing knowledge, I knew that such a pang of discomfort could only be a sign of regurgitation. I flounced to the bathroom, and in only a second after squatting down, facing the toilet seat, I puked. I started palpitating and shivering. Every sphere I came into contact with, as I walked towards my room, felt unfriendly to all my senses. I was weak!

Coco asked calmly, but solemnly, "MrSir, what's wrong? You freaking me out. One - your room is almost empty. Two - you throwing up and ish... What happened to your clothes? What have you eaten?"

Had my mouth not been full of saliva, my attempt to respond would have been a success. I became impatient with myself. I started pouring tears and snorting mucus onto the tissue that Coco offered when she thought that I was stoically unwilling to open up despite my condition. I thought it was my time. "Am I even ready?" The moment I asked myself that question, I immediately switched its concept to whether I'll be ready for my class or not.

My toes towed my heels towards my bed and with a great sigh, sprang my whole body onto my bed. I gave my wristwatch a quick peep and concluded that it was already late. I failed to peel off all the elements that impeded me from gaining strength for attending that class. So I turned a blank thought to regrets.

They offered me all the help within their reach, and in my thankful response, I only pleaded for some 'me - time'. My roommate joined his girlfriend for a night or two, if not more. I surrendered myself to my lonely room when they reluctantly departed.

Could I have heard that? Of course, I could! Tell you what - it was a sound of a big city, Johannesburg. I heard the harmonies of big cemented trees whistling, conversations in different languages, cars hooting, juveniles squealing in delight, different genres of music playing- it was a compound of various tunes, each one attaining its composition throughout the entire interference.

My ears went selective. I projected my heed to accents of people who spoke English. You'd bet that ninety per cent of them were coconuts. They sounded as though they were trying hard to - if not only by looks and sounds - feel white.

When I was listening to fading voices, I could barely sieve words and tones of young people from those of older ones. The city was constituted of people with different ages, characters and interests, but with the same mission. It was a city of Gold, of course, so the mission was related to either making money or reaching success of some sort.

I nodded off right in the middle of my philosophies, and dreamed about nothing worth remembering. A call startled me, and before I could even answer, I yawned and checked the time. My mind was telling me that I had a class to attend. It was a different number, and surely a different person.

"MrSir - Hello?" I answered.

"Hi, I'm sorry for bothering you this late, but I need to know this -" she said, sighing slowly. Her voice was calm, collected and patient. She could steal any busy man's heed by just exhaling few words.

She continued by asking for my real name and whether it was me who came to her institution before the long weekend. I replied honestly and confirmed that it was me, but I also wondered if it was her whom I gazed at. It wasn't the first time we spoke, but we'd never met until...

I asked if we could meet on a Saturday and she agreed. "This is my mom's phone, please don't call it. I'll buzz you with my new number just now," she insisted. That explained why I didn't recognize the number and why her old number wasn't answered when I tried to call.

After hanging up, reality hit my worries and curiosities. "Who could've done that though? How did they disappear? How did they even get into this building? How did they know that I wouldn't be in my room?" I asked myself. Part of me suspected the security guy's involvement. I said a short prayer in my heart, hoping my feet won't fail me as I attempted to lean on the headboard. I stood up, tiptoed and bounced up and down like a boxer, you know? Measured the Joules I possessed, you know? Kind of feeling strong and healthy, you know?

A lightning of concern stroke my thoughts, "The security guy!" Then I expected my legs to carry me all the way downstairs. They were strong! You bet they were stronger that Muhammad Ali's fists and faster than how he claimed to be, when he said, "I'm so fast that when I switch off the lights, I get to bed before they go out. Bad! I'm that fast!"

As I sprinted out of my room, I thought to myself, "I have to confront him. Surely he was involved." When I approached the elevator, my heels passed their responsibility onto my knees, and they made me grind to a crawl just when I was about to stop it.

(Do you know how it feels when you are in the middle of a very steamed conversation on Mxit, WhatsApp - any other Social Network or a phone call - then without a warning - data, airtime or battery dies? Yeah, that's a perfect analogy!)

There was a sudden drain of energy and my knees got weak in a nick of time. That speed? The strength - were all temporary, sort of an adrenalin rush. You would even suspect that I was on either drugs or energy boosters. My feet failed me right at the elevator's door! I translated my focus towards recuperating again, and obliviously forgot why I initially wanted to go downstairs.

I crawled back to my room, consumed the remnants of fast food that I had for supper the previous night and went back to bed. I didn't really have much appetite, but my digestive system had to be kept busy with something. While in bed, few seconds before I attempted to dream, I remembered that I had a class to facilitate at home, M´villa, and a date the following day. So I set my alarm to wake me up early.

"But the security guy!" a part of me remarked. "Ah - well, I'll see him when I return from home," another part of me replied.

I planned how I'll replace the stolen clothes and shoes without asking for anyone's help, simply because I had an intense dislike for pity. Then I hummed my favorite gospel song (*Bonang Ho hlahileng Marung*, directly translated from Setswana: Look what appeared from the clouds) at a very low pitch until I passed out.

Chapter B - Blessing, a Break from the mystery.

Tring - Tring! Tring - Tring!

"MrSir - Hello?" I answered.

"Peace unto you," my father greeted.

He woke me up a bit earlier than my set - alarm. After all those typical greetings, he asked if I was still going home despite how bad the weather was, at home. I had to persist, so I said that whatever weather, home was where I was heading to.

It was at the heart of May, but as cold as July. The sleet was actually pelting down, but I still persisted. I guess my determination, along with the presence of the Supreme Being, were my panaceas. I was just so healthy that you would even doubt my previous day's state. I took a quick shower and did the usual, then in less than a duration equivalent to an eighth of a day, I was facilitating at my former high school.

My body was in that class, my mind was in it too, but my dissociated heart was impatient with the feeling of 'finally going to see her'. I always delayed class dismissals due to further explanations and emphasis on contents of the subject, but that day 'time is out' meant exactly that!

"MrSir, please don't forget to sign. Where are we rushing off to?" said the prefect.

"Thanks mama! Well - home. There's no place like it. Is there?" I replied vaguely and we just smiled. She could tell that I was in a rush, but my typical character of not sharing plans and occurrences of my life with anyone stood in her way of asking further questions. My mentees and learners knew when and what to and not to ask, especially when it came to me.

After signing the register, I went straight home. I dropped my bags, greeted my folks and cousins in jubilation and in a rush for a continuation of attending errands, then came back to catch a taxi to her hood. We discussed through a call about where I was supposed to disembark before I made a 'pointing down finger' sign for a taxi to decelerate to a halt so that I could embark. I took off precisely where we agreed to meet, but I had to wait for at most a twelfth of an hour before she could show up. Before she did, I still had to walk a little so as to meet her half way.

As I approached, there she was - wrapped up like a Christmas gift, and the whole package was merry. With her little yellow face peeping out of her beanie, her tiny tawny hands intermittently seeking heat from her jacket pockets, and her chin disappearing behind the sash of her bottleneck. It was flipping cold, yet she managed to constantly look hot! She - was - beautiful!

My hair repelled from my skin, pulled by the force of attraction that existed between us. Indeed we were unlike charges! Just a simple 'Hi' hug gave me instant goosebumps. I was really charged, and I mean REALLY CHARGED. 'It' (the mini me) got happy and reacted, but I used her oblivion as a broom to sweep off 'its' excitement.

In the process of complimenting her, words rejected my sincere plead for being precise and synergic, 'cause they weren't modifying even half of the description of her beauty and charisma...

No rain formed against us prospered. Instead, it pinched a little romance upon our kiss - a very intimate, breathtaking and blood boiling kiss. Her strength of luring me was an accident arising from my weakness of having already been captivated. I had smears of affection all over my face, which became quite a herd of elephants the moment I emphasized my seriousness. I was allowing myself to trip while enjoying our bond-formation.

After few 'forevers', lost in the 'situation right now', our hallucinations were wrenched from our fantasy world by an old lady, walking past us with a juvenile. They seemed to try heaving their heed away from us. I passed a derisive greeting to them, prodding their awareness of disturbing us. Of course it was a public place, but who said public places couldn't be aligned with privacy?

Having such antagonistic thoughts, I whispered into her left ear, "What do you think they could be doing here?"

"Mm! I have no idea," was her whisper in response. I then separated my mind and my flesh, leaving my flesh all over her, and my mind trying to figure out what business could people possibly have had at a small mountain that was in such an open space.

Pankop and M'villa were blessed with the beauty of such small mountains – they had two of them. Pankop's landscape was suitable for a formal settlement, but unfortunately Pankop and M'villa were both developing villages at the time, situated in the shallow part of Mpumalanga Province – the first places to intersect with when you exited Gauteng Province. Basically, Blessing's geographic background was same as mine.

In a trice, her scent managed to cease my curiosities and caught my psychological attention. It was a very pleasurable aroma for one's nostrils. With her portable figures, and her complementing beautiful facial features, her scent confirmed that I was indeed holding a rose.

On the basis that I had sluggish legs, I glanced for a small stone to perch on. Due to low temperatures, I offered her my laps. Not only to exchange heat and to rest her legs too, but to also cuddle and be as close as possible.

We did not really talk much. Our efforts were put more on sharing the valence electrons of every building atom of our flesh, than on expressing our minds.

"What are your intentions with me?" she asked.

"Sweetness, intentions are practically expectations. I am just in the moment, blindly hoping for the better. Question is: what do you hope for?" was my response.

"Eh! I really don't know," she dilated her eyelids and gave me a surreptitious glance.

I had to ease the tension, so I quickly said, "In actual fact, I enjoy consorting with you. I would be even more content and jubilant if you allowed you and I to be us. When considering the idea that we are a good match that will always ignite the same spark, I have no choice but to ask for your permission to give it a try..."

She was censored and I thought it best to just go for what we did best, a vacuum kiss that time! We stood up and gave each other a very tight hug, and pierced each other with a very bond forming eye contact. Then we started kissing...

Our tongues locked, our lips overlapped, our jaws dropped allowing enough sucking and proper inhalation, our noses flipped against each other, my hands were all over her... It was as if it would go down right there!

Her femora climbed up around my waist, her shins crossing over my tail bone, my hands framing her hips and thighs by holding and slithering them. You'd reckon it was a very intimate moment. We felt no loss of heat anymore as if we had reached equilibrium. Just being filed against each other was enough to secure our energies from being gravitated by the surrounding.

Oops! The isolated system was grinded to a blow by a cavalcade of cattle successing past a metre away from us. With a sigh, recovering from 'you know what', I made a claim, "Wait! You know? I have a mutual understanding with cattle. They could hear me quite well if I attempted to converse with them."

"No ways!"

"Okay then, check this out," I intended to prove it.

I faced them and whistled in different tunes. Coincidentally, they stopped and turned their heads to me as if they were paying attention. I took pride in their coordination and whistled a placid tune that time, lowering the intonations, and they dispersed making sounds (Mooo!) as if they were responding. It seemed too convenient that even an obstinate person would have bought it. I guess coincidence was the root of all evil, huh?

"Wow! You - are - something else!" She squeezed her cheeks with her palms, opening her mouth - looking quite astonished.

"Well, not even philosophy can explain that, can it?" I then told her that all those reactions were completely coincidental. I also told her that I was just kidding. Had I not come clean, she'd have believed that I really could talk to cattle. "Pshhh! What a talent to claim." I thought to myself. Well - coincidence was, after all, a major building block for false prophesies.

I switched from that lousy joke to expressing myself. I bet the pleasure I got from seeing her blush when I told her how beautiful she was, was greater than the pleasure she got from blushing. I utilized all the opportunities that I had, to make her feel special. Not because it was my job to, but because she was indeed special. Although giving her all the grandeur she deserved wasn't the focal point, being the fervent lover that I was, an incline in her significance in my life exponentially sloped up in proportion to the quantity of time I spent on conversing with her, and thinking about her.

Her eyeballs would pop out every time when I said, "I think my emotions are getting involved now. I doubt I'm not falling for you."

To confess, I preferred logical double negations. I'd deliberately construct a phrase in a cryptic manner just to suck the efforts of analyzing out of her. Part of me knew that she wasn't up for anything serious yet. In actual fact, she thought I wasn't serious too. I could eavesdrop into her paralinguistic gestures when I asked about her willingness to reach the plateau with me.

However, my impatient patience enabled me to hoist her from her initial ideas up to reality. Since I had always known that grapevines already led her astray by introducing me with fallacies, I had to shape my salutations in such a way that will draw her attention towards what was real and true. That was when I realized that:

Word For The Record: If it's not from the horse's mouth, then it's belittled, exaggerated or not true at all. One should always question the authority of sources before they assimilate, adhere to and spread their messages. It's rumor if it's not directly from the owner.

In the middle of our small Question-and-Answer session, I digressed with gratitude, "Without sounding too sure, I'd like to acknowledge your contribution in cutting off the branches of all grapevines carrying my name, and thank you for giving me a chance to express myself. It really is a great honor to be assessed by having my body territory penetrated. I can only hope that what you were mostly told contradict what you observed and discovered by yourself."

She nodded in response and just smiled away. She never really said much. Instead, she'd just hide her face inside her palms and availed it for casual kisses. I'd say that she was shy if I didn't know better. Coming to think of it, maybe she was, or maybe she was just being coy. Either way, no composure impeded her from hurling few jokes onto our moods and dropping thin punch-lines out of teasing upon my astonishments. She was quite fun to be around.

We were caught up in a moment to an extent that grass started growing under our feet.

"Mhm! Babe, the road I'm forced to use to get to grand mom's place is quite atrocious. I won't manage passing through it if we depart later than now - I hate to go but... damn! I'm really gonna miss you, a lot!" she said and sighed, while giving me the tightest and warmest hug the whole earth had never offered.

We held hands and trotted to the outline. In less than ten minutes, we were in a taxi. Before I could even memorize her face, she had already called the driver to a halt, given me a chaste kiss on the cheek and disembarked. I gazed at her fading image through the windowpane as the driver changed gears real quick. I was happy with what I had, but sad for what I couldn't spend more time with. It felt like I was seeing her for the last time. Then I told myself that, it was only the beginning of a 'forever' moment. She was a complete piece of my missing rib.

Chapter C - Conceived a Child through a Contraceptive?

T hat - was - quite - a digression from all the cryptic ironies of life! In the middle of the reminiscence over how tremendous my day was, passing the 'short left' corner - where I was supposed to have taken off - patted my awareness of being in a taxi and ceased the trip I took down the memory lane. I then disembarked at the following bus stop which was about sixteen metres away from where I should've taken off. I still managed to see myself arriving home without feeling the remoteness.

I went straight to my bedroom and paged through my recent poetry journal. It was when I came across one of the pieces of art I wrote when I was a little hurt from one of my past relationships, yet still hopeful for future romance, when my creativity knocked for a new poem. It was the first poem I performed live at Ram Jam, SABC Stages.

The title of the poem was: *WHAT I FEEL*, and it went like this...

It seems as though that love
is nothing but the hatred above
all that one had ever had.
Pretty much as the absence of gloves
when in contact with the H-I-Virus
it is how it leaves you hurt.

All those happy and special moments,
all those plights and predicaments.
As ironic as they can all sound,
it is on their grounds-

that we say we want to fall in it,
thinking it is a pleasurable pit,
blind to see that it is just a slit,
pouring blood out of one's heart.

I want to be loved to the core

until it feels like hatred is no more
in my heart. Only love should bore
deep into my chest, until I get a love-ore.

Is there anything that must be done,
for me to be with that only one,
who can fit perfectly like she's my clone,
and support me like my skeletal bone?

We are contingent on its existence.
It is a tool for men's diligence.
But once we give it to one for a sip,
life gets tougher than a pouting lip.

Shouldn't we feel love before;
we hear about it?
Shouldn't it be given to those;
who never doubt it?

I don't wanna fall for someone;
out of justification and will.
Instead, I wanna be mute as an;
explanation for What I Feel!

The day's inspiration was quite a good kick to my creativity. So I happened to have written a new one which I planned to share with her after few weeks of having gotten to know her. Although, being honest with myself, it was 'so far so good'.

Her temperament corresponded with my personality. It was like God made her just for me. Her body was like a 'key-to-its-lock' to my arms - fitted perfectly! Her beauty was as concave as my spectacles - complementary to my eyes! You'd even bet that Photoshop was programmed just to align other people's beauty with hers - and guess what - they never got any close. Her... (Okay - I can go on the whole day or write the whole story describing her if I don't stop now.)

By the time I finished that poem, the sun had already disappeared to the other side of earth. Since it was cloudy, its light (reflected by the moon) did not shine upon our heads. It was dark as hell! Well, the concept of hell being dark made a pinch of a topic for the rest of the evening. I wondered how it would be dark if there was an eternal flame there.

Immediately when I finished writing that poem, I text notified her about my late call, then exited my room. Just when my face collided with the aroma in the dining room, before my nostrils could utilize the pleasure, my ears were gravitated by "Uwahaa! Eh! Mr. KIA (Know It All), what you saying again?" which escaped one of my cousin's loud mouth. When they saw me, they invited me to the table. It was more of an invitation to the topic than it was to food.

I sat, said a short prayer in my heart, and helped myself with my preferable relish only. As I was digging in, I had already understood where the topic was going, and tell you what - they were arguing about how the 'Holy Bible' described hell. It was three of them, one was two years younger than me, the second one was my age and the last one was four years older than me (the one they called Mr. KIA). In the core of the informal debate, my older cousin said, "Earth as it is, is hell."

That, on its own, raised my eyebrows without giving out a disdainful remark. You see - my cousin was a Sunday School Teacher. So referencing him would be a relevant appeal to authority. Even though he would sometimes propose invalid arguments with illogical premises based on his beliefs, I would still not oppose openly.

I was one person who did not want to offend people by attacking their religious beliefs as much as I was protective over mine.

Word For The Record: 'People's values are just as important to them as yours are to you, and there is no such thing as some values being better than others.' - Business Communication in Business Management.

Instead of opposing, I asked, "Is hell a dark place or a lightened up place? What's the source of the eternal fire that's burning there?"

He answered, "The fire spoken about in the Bible is not a visible fire. It's a spiritual fire solely made for the souls of sinners." After that, I was so ready for him, without intending on offending him.

I had compiled a series of questions in my mind, and asked further without breathing, "So if earth is hell, does that mean everyone who goes to heaven must have been in hell before? What about Jerusalem? Was it a place on earth, what you call hell, or was it also a spiritual land which wasn't visible?

Okay - Let's talk about Jesus, was He sent to hell? Jesus was in hell? Or let's rather heed this one: If the lives of those who steal, hate and kill are so nice here on earth, and the lives of saints are so difficult, does that mean hell is good for sinners? Wasn't hell built for eternal punishment? Last one please - Are we living in the first, last, or post chapters of Revelations?" Then I sighed heavily.

For some reasons I knew no one would answer my questions in a contentious way, and I was too obstinate to even allow anyone to try - but I was open for a debate. I was not an expert in religion, but I was very quick to ask questions whenever someone presented themselves as experts. Somehow, in my heart, I believed that we had different perceptions and values as people. Our values and perceptions were built on our past experiences, and since we experienced different things - most of the times when our values clashed, we would not be willing to give in to someone else's values - we would rather stick to ours and expect others to join.

My cousin was quite smart. Sometimes I believed he was smarter than me, he was older than me, so I expected him to be smarter than me - however, his belief systems made me question his brains - although he would argue that I was mentally strong, but spiritually weak - I could not argue because until one of us died before, our arguments would still be based on mere speculations, perceptions and values, and like I said, we differed a lot in regard to those concepts. To be fair - we were both smart, but as for spirituality - we just had different belief systems.

After a series of my questions - there was a pin drop silence for few seconds. They all gazed at me, and the attention was so piercing that

I had no choice but to continue digging in. Plus - my food was losing heat (getting cold, so they said).

"*Yoh*! You can talk a blue streak when you want, *neh*?" my peer cousin remarked. They were really astonished. Not only by the number of questions I asked, but by the fact that I made my older cousin's jaw drop. He was shut until I left the table.

(Well - don't get me wrong. I also had the KIA tendencies. I was just not ready to give anyone my spot. I guess we shared that in common, me and him. Not fair? Was I a hypocrite? Whatever! I was just being human!)

When they started dipping into other silly and pointless topics, I was already full. So I remembered that I had few documents to file and a report to write. I went back to my bedroom and worked.

Before dozing, I called Blessing, and we spoke for almost an hour and a half. Should I, perhaps, say, I spoke for an hour? 'Cause I did more talking than she did. Not that she was quiet - she was just adapting to my level of craziness.

After bidding each other a 'goodnight', I almost slept like a baby without saying my prayers, until the mysterious girl's number decided to come back into my phone's received calls.

Just when everything seemed normal again, after moving on, ready to go back to Jo'burg the following day for a new start, she felt the need to contaminate my new beginning. An incoming call from her number lit my screen at around ten minutes to twelve post meridiem.

"*Hola* stranger, will you tell me who you are today and stop playing games?" I answered.

"*Ekse my broer*, *wat soek jy* from my girl? *Hoekom jy* doing this to her? To us?" said - a - guy.

I expected a girl. To my surprise, it was her mixed race boyfriend who mixed English and Afrikaans in her citations! (AKA: Coloured boyfriend, in South Africa.)

"Sorry *broer, maar* who is your girl? What's her *naam*?" I indulged in his accent and tone, thinking I was making my message clear, only to realize that I was drawing curses and threats. Along the phrases he spat, he accused me of being a racist, an opportunist, not to forget a coward too!

I was tired from the long day I had, I didn't have any energy for him. So I just hung up.

Few seconds after telling myself that I had to put that number on reject list, I received a text message from a number I didn't know. It said,

"Hello, MrSir. My daughter had long confirmed that her current boyfriend is not the father. She is three months old now, so you can do the math. MrSir, she deserves to know her father. I trust that you are smart enough to know what to do. I really apologize on her behalf for being stubborn, selfish and reckless. She told me what happened for you to be the father...

Kind regards,
Basetsana's mother."

I felt like I could just switch off and wake up in a different world. Whoa! Not in a suicidal way - as in - a different situation. I just couldn't believe my eyes!

"Basi was pregnant? Carrying my child? Why didn't she tell me? *Jah neh*!" I thought to myself.

I tried to add one and two to get four, but it gave me three. I wanted the results to favor me, but no theory helped me surmise anything. I guess that was just not how reality worked. One plus two would always give me three.

Word For The Record: Expectation is a building block of disappointment. Acceptance is the key to happiness. When you add one and two to get four, you disregard reality. Rather forget four and work with the three that you get! Don't align your wishes with just your expectations, align them with reality.

I tried calling Basi, but she rejected my call and decided to text this to me, "*I don't want you near my child, period! And don't try contacting me again.*"

Eh! I tried again, and her eerie boyfriend picked it up.

"Ai! Not you again," I said, and hung up. That's when I realized what the early call I received was about.

I guess my reaction to him 'answering Basie's phone' kind of perturbed him, giving him the onus to call back and inflected in his curtailed speech, "My *broer*, you see *ek*? *Ek* don't mind raising her. *Ek kan* take care of them, *ek is lief vir* (I love) them my *broer*! *Jy forr staan*? *Ek* took her as my daughter, my *broer*. She wants nothing to do with you, she said it! She still feels bad about how you guys ended things, how she played and hurt you. *Maar sy ma* (but her mother) wants you to take over. *Hoekom* (why)? *Hoekom* my *broer*? *Hoekom* are you people doing this to my family? I love them, my *broer*! Wit' all my heart. I just wanna continue raising her as my kid. *Maar ek weet* that *ek* can't if you wanna take over. *Hoekom my broer*? Which man sprays a girl, not forgive her for one mistake and come back for his baby? Which man does that my *broer*? My *broer*, please let's not complicate things and just let me raise her. *Ek is lief vir* her, *my broer*! Please *praat* wit' her *ma*, please!"

I was speechless and ambivalent. I didn't know what to say, what to think, what to do with the situation, how to feel about it, whether to try and understand or not, - in a nutshell, my confusion was abysmal that it became very unlikely of me to sound preposterous in my response. Not to forget, short too.

Without violating the rules of etiquette, a short phrase that everyone used when they were speechless saved me, "Well - let me think about it. I'll get back to you." Then I hung up before he could say one more *'broer'*.

In my mind, these questions boiled my neurotransmitters to an extent that I attracted a severe headache,

"Three months old? I have a daughter and I didn't know? Why are they telling me now? How did it happen? This must be a prank! Wait - But I'm always protected! How long had her mom known? I'm a father? Hehehe! Basetsana *neh*... Basie has a child? My child? This - Must - Be - A - Nightmare!"

I gave my pillow a tight fist of three punches just to let it all out. I felt like I could explode, as if all that was not real. I pinched the skin that was covering the triceps on my left arm, and the little pain resulted startled me. Indeed I was wide awake! Since my life had always been complex, resulting in my low retention, I always planned things by writing them down.

The system served as intrapersonal communication, and the paper was my memory. I took a pen and a book from my headboard, and tried to plan how I'd deal with it. Unfortunately it was neither like a rider from Euclidean Geometry, nor was it like integrating trigonometric inverse ratios. It wasn't that simple!

C++ Coding and Programming was far too easy compared to the complexity of the situation. Yes! Even a balance sheet was not complex - balancing chemical equations too. Not to forget Technical Drawing (EGD). They were all easy compared to the situation...

What was going on in my life then, required only the Supreme Being's level of comprehension. God Himself!

So I got off my bed, dropped the pen and kneeled down facing the left width of my bed. The scriptures said that God already knew what we wanted long before we were conceived, so I always saw no point of making a long pray saying which described my demands word by word, no matter how rough times were. I had an everyday prayer that I always said, which I wrote and constructed with my heart and mind - coalesced. It went like this...

God of Abraham, God of Isaac and God of Jacob, I come before You my Lord, as humble and tiny as a simple particle - to give You all the glory that exist in this world, and in Heaven, to give You all gratitude for all that were given to us, Your children, by You, our Father. To give You all the praises that art, poetry and wordplay can't outshine. To plead You for a list of our needs and wants, not forgetting wisdom, knowledge and understanding, including peace and love to reign.

The needs being, life itself, shelter, food, water, health and a good, productive company - be it healthy relationships with good friends, family members, neighbors, colleagues and our companions. Grant us all our wishes my Lord, answer all our prayers, give us all the necessary strength to prosper, succeed and make it through all obstacles. Be merciful to us, ignorant sinners, and forgive us our oblivious deeds.

Give us the heart of Your Son, the wealth of Abraham, the gifts of Joseph, and the leadership skills of Moses, most importantly the ability to comprehend and connect with Your Word and Your Holy Spirit. Rehabilitate us who are addicted to sin, guide us who do not see the light, talk to us who don't know the truth, heal us who are sick and give life to us who are dead. Take our will, my Lord, and teach us Yours. Take our language, and teach us Yours. For Your will is the only way, and Your language of Love is life.

Redirect us away from atrocious accidents, keep us out of hospitals, give us good judgement against deceivers, protect us from negative energies and feed our minds, our senses and possessions with what we desire and long to receive at all times. Bless us my Lord. I humble myself before you in the name of the Father, the Son and the Holy Spirit. Oh! Our Father, who art in Heaven...

It was around Four ante meridiem when I went back to sleep. To lull myself, as I was slowly closing my eyes, my brain automatically reminisced over how painful and sombre my break up with Basie was. I knew we were never going to be together again, but the child still needed both her parents. I slept knowing that I would do everything in my capabilities to be part of my daughter's life.

Chapter D – Dichotomization of Basetsana and I.

Basetsana was a very beautiful young lady - short, with visible arcs, light-skinned, with pure-white Chinese eyes, moderate-sized lips, with round behinds but slim waist, with long hair, and her nose was - well, was - let me just say unique and beautiful. Yes, her nose was unique and beautiful, that's how I saw it. She used to think that I was teasing her whenever I praised it, but I was always rather genuine than being a sycophant.

Our dates weren't bad at all, in fact, I enjoyed her company. She was a master in coaxing, but I never questioned anything. We were peers, but she was only a student with no part-time jobs of some sort. She was entirely financially contingent on her folk's contributions. She was adventurous, but never loaded. So I had to always dip into my pockets for all our adventures.

She was smart, eloquent, intermittently hilarious, had an exquisite sense of humor, could sing for days, dance for years, argue for decades, ... All that, explained why I took her serious after meeting her. We were really exhaustive and mutually exclusive - yes! We were complementary pieces!

Reminiscing over how we met, it was on a Saturday morning, around nine ante meridiem. I had a class to facilitate at a township called Mabopane (just outside the West side of Pretoria), and I traveled straight from Jozi (Johannesburg). I bumped into her in front of Hungry Lion Restaurant at Bloed Street, Pretoria CBD. She was about to step past the door, into the restaurant - No, wait. She was actually about to think of stepping in - Noo! (Let me give it one last shot...)

She was standing in front of the door, yes! Just standing in front of it, waiting for her homosexual friend to finish doing whatever he was doing with his phone.

My eyes were subtended by her 'back', and I kind of stared. I didn't think at the time. Maybe being a male species took over my hormonal reactions and my pituitary gland was prodded into doing its job. So 'it' reacted a little and deterred me from trotting. My problem was that 'its' reaction was visible to any observant person, and it always took me at most forty Seconds before I could be myself again.

I stared as I approached her, and my sight was disturbed by a sudden appearance of her friend's hand waving in my face.

"Hell-low, Perv'! You'll end up tripping over what ain't yours," her friend said.

His face was distorted with grimace, but he turned to call her, smiling. I was embarrassed and tried to calm 'it' down. My 'game' crushed my attempt of apologizing.

Before she could arrive at our spot, I had to apply one of the rules of ´game´, which was to be favored by her friends and folks, no matter how difficult or boring they may had seemed or sounded.

So I said, softly, "Is it my eyes or *vele* it's you? I mean, I can't be homo..."

"Wait! Watchu on about?" he asked, looking perplexed and trying to figure out what I implied.

"Don't get me wrong hey, I'm straight. But - that doesn't have to stop me from acknowledging beauty when I see one, right? Even when that beauty is possessed by - gays? I just hope your friendship with her is not based on the idea of 'we are both hot, so why not?' I mean, I'm just saying..." I added some sauce.

It wasn't easy to pitch a light compliment without misleading him, but I could only hope for better results. He blushed in gratitude and temporarily forgot his intentions of calling her.

Phew! At least I had already won her friend's platonic preference, and I was willing to search all the nooks and crannies to win her heart. She had that thing, you know? That ngrrrr! The sauce! In a nutshell, she was the female version of me. How did I know? Well, I knew she was one I had to be with when she, without hiding, approached us while checking me out. And I mean, CHECKING ME OUT. Yes, she saw 'it'. I bet she was as naughty as she was beautiful! She checked the 'print'. Her eyes pierced every organ eyes of any naughty person would subtend, and smiled as she got closer and closer.

The moment she arrived, I WAS CAPTIVATED. She was gorgeous! Her face, her hair, her body, Oh-Yes! Her smile could attract a blind man, and deceive a Bishop. Wait until I get to her voice, mhmmm! Beyoncé The Legacy! I was a young adult, so I was easily charmed.

I kept my composure and told her friend that I was in a hurry for my appointment without calculating. In response, he said, "But - you haven't met my friend. Basie, this is -"

"MrSir," I completed the introduction, having known that we didn't exchange names.

Then he continued, "Yes, the funny 'MrSir' in flesh. I have you on Facebook! Wow! THIS IS A SMALL WORLD. He's quite a catch though, ain't he *chomi*?" he remarked, glancing at Basie and winked, then looked at me to continue, "MrSir, this is Basie, a very 'packed' and hot friend of mine," he put his hand on his right cheek, as if he was trying to block sound waves from reaching Basie's ears, and completed his phrase in a whisper, "and she's single."

When he said 'packed', he quoted it with his index fingers, reminding me of my early actions. I was oblivious to the reminder, for few seconds. A microscopic inch of my cheeks turned red for a moment when I caught the glimpse. He was a benign person, bubbly for centuries and seemed to enjoy pairing people. Maybe that was just how it was for people like him. Since their complementary pairs were scarce, it was rather more fun for them to pair others. And - They were quite good at both pairing and separating, you bet! If you weren't in their good books, you wouldn't dare hit on their friends. Thank God I wasn't homophobic!

"Hell-low MrSir, why don't we just have lunch together? Delayed breakfast, perhaps? Since it's not yet twelve. Yes? No? Maybe? Or your girl is waiting for you?" she tested me, but I was game for all of it.

It felt like she knew that I had to meet up with someone first (before facilitating), but hey, it could have also been her game! Either way, that 'someone' wasn't worth not losing at the time, so I took the plunge. I thought I had 'not much' to lose. You bet after cancelling the appointment with that 'someone' in my heart, alone, I was then not in a hurry anymore. I still had two full blown hours in my hands.

I said, "If you knew that I'm an artist, you wouldn't have asked. You would have just told me. Unless if you were being rhetoric, weren't you?"

She tried to dilate the spaces between her eyelids in surprise, but the efforts made no difference to their natural shape.

She then said, "Mm! I'm - drawing - blank! Please give it a scale factor of a positive integer!" (Which meant: 'Please stretch your point, I don't get it.') I was hooked by her wordplay.

"Which artist would turn down the offer of having lunch with the personification of art herself?" I tried to add more emphasis with a little bit of more ngrrr! Just to stretch the compliment. She couldn't hide that she was taken too, but wouldn't let me win her over that easy.

She found a way of flipping the page and went back to her question, "Soo - MrSir, are you also hungry? Because I am," and she rolled her eyes.

"I still have few minutes of witnessing such beauty hey, and few seconds of allowing my ears to feel the pleasure of the melody in your voice. Soo - I'd just use this lunch-or-breakfast as a bridge. Shall we?" I offered her my inequality-shaped left elbow in an impetuous and natural way that I subdued her reluctance. She hung hers around it and we made our way into the restaurant as if we were already an item. Maybe we were...

"*Chomi, somaar* you'll be able to settle your accounts in the meantime - *wabon'* (yousee)? Unless if you don't mind the heat of this burning wick. Do you?" she said.

I stood inert for a moment, stunned by her considerable intellect.

She continued, "What? Or you want her to join us?" She was wondering why I gazed at her with my eyebrows squeezed.

I then noted the 'her' in her question and learned that most homosexual male people considered themselves ladies, so there was no need for 'he/his/him' in my previous citations. From then, her friend was a she. As long as the pronoun is not used as a tease!

I answered her, "Not really, it's not that. Ever heard of BWB? Beauty With Brains? Well - let's just go and order hey... Oh and," I turned to face her friend, continuing, "...it was nice meeting you."

Basie's eyes sparkled and shone with contentment. I had forgotten to ask who was going to pay for our lunch, but having enough cash with me made me give in to the idea of 'just be the man and pay'.

Her friend said, "Burning wick doesn't beat what ya'll be producing. This one is a primus stove! Hai - lemme just give ya'll some space neh, and MrSir, take care of my friend... Otherwise - nice meeting you too. Later, -*Chomz*!"

Our sounds lightly seeped out of our lungs through our tracheas in a reluctant laughter. Then we saw our way into the restaurant. As we got closer and closer to the counter, I asked, "Tell me - are you a writer of some sort?"

"Uhm - it takes one to see one, right? Oh and I'm not asking, I'm -"

"- telling," we said the last continuous verb simultaneously and smiled. It was like we had known each other for years. Completing each other's sentences became a norm to us since then. She had a retentive memory and could make sense of most of my cryptic philosophies. She understood me quite fast! I officially cancelled my 'supposed to have been my appointment' through a text before we made our way to the tables, after ordering. That was how we met...

Fast forward, to the core of events - on the sixth month of our relationship. I had already met her parents, and they took me as their son. Coming to think of it, they would actually ask me to rebuke Basie on their behalf whenever she acted 'somehow' or 'funny' at home. I was a good boy to them, kind of a potential *'mogonyana'* (son-in-law), I could say...

Did I mention that we always used protection? In fact, I never indulged in not using it with anyone. So one evening when she was in my room for few days of sleeping over, she said, "I wanna know how it feels to be sprayed. We'll buy MAPs (Morning After Pills) tomorrow." Women and their unscrupulous adventure tendencies!

"Nah bayb', that's not gonna happen. I thought we spoke about this hao - It's risky and we not ready to raise a child. We can't allow a few seconds of pleasure ruin our future hey. I mean, don't you believe our future is worth the wait? A little patience won't hurt, Sweetness," I solemnly said, patting her shoulder softly.

She always mentioned that we'd make good genes for our kids, that we'd either reproduce beautiful girls or handsome boys. Even though she used to sound more frivolous than earnest in her tone, she still used to mention it frequently. But - I never heeded her determination.

We were barely financially stable to bring a child into this world, and we were still studying for crying out loud! To be point-blank, we had all convenient and logical premises to support this conclusion: We could not afford to have children. Well - at least that was what I thought. Were we on the same page? I could only hope!

I never wanted us to fall out over such an insignificant matter, and neither did she over anything. So she just went down on me, helped me with the wrapper and we went for the last round of the evening. (Too much information? Well...)

The following day, I woke up a little late, got out of bed as fast as I could while she was still in her dreams, took a ten-to-fifteen-minutes shower and hurried out to Campus for only important early classes. I didn't follow my daily routines, for I had planned a nice surprise for her. Guess What? It was indeed a surprise! An unfavorable surprise for both of us!

I returned to my room Four hours prior to my typical time of returning. I wanted to spend more time with her since she was going back to school (Pretoria) the following day.

I had bought JC La'roux Non-alcoholic wine (Blush) and Tennis Choc-mint Biscuits for starters, two McDonald's Double Quarter Pounders and Red Tisersfor lunch, Strawberries, Ferrero Rocher chocolates, Ultra Mel Vanilla Custard and Fresher Choc-mint Ice-cream for dessert. For appearance, I purchased Colored Pillar Candles and a bouquet of roses.

After exiting the elevator, walking towards my room's door, I called her, "My Danone, the salt to my tea and the sugar to my scrambled eggs, it's going down tod-"

Just when I was about to finish saying the word 'today', after opening the door, I COULD NOT BELIEVE MY EYES. It was indeed a surprise! She didn't expect all that, she didn't expect me to be back that early as well. I stood motionless at the door, dropped my jaw, squeezed my eyebrows, sighed and palpitated.

She quickly put her hands on her mouth, and swallowed words. The guy put his hands on his head, followed by, "Eish! Yoh!" They were nude, and seemed to have been half way there...

All her attempts of showing remorse failed as I was pissed and hurt.

I caught her red handed! Not anywhere, but in my room. Not on the floor, but in my bed. Not on the mattress, but in my blankets! I was almost destroyed. It was like she did that each day I was out.

The nerve and the liver she had were those of wild animals! I felt used and played. "Condolences was better," I thought to myself, "at least she always came clean," I consoled myself. I chased them out of my room, promising them trouble if I were to see them again in my life. I made it very clear to her that she was dead to me on that day, that I cursed the day I met her.

After a week or so, she tried to get hold of me, claiming to have "something important to talk to me about", claiming to "have changed" and claiming to have been "sorry" - but I was not willing to let her back into my life. She then threw in the towel by confessing a part of her evil deed. She told me that she took advantage of the love I had for her to get what she wanted, and that she finally got it.

I didn't care about her aims. I just tried to move on. The rest was Algebra!

After few months of trying to move on, I wrote a poem out of anger. It simply emphasized how women thought men didn't have feelings and emotions. How they thought that we were just 'Balls of Cells that have no love'.

So I dedicated it to Basetsana, expressing my anger...

The Title of the poem was: *Balls Of Cells That Have No Love*, and it went like this...

I'm feeling like a material,
kind of a source of an income,
you bet to them we really are,
balls of cells that have no love.

Shhh! A moment of silence for
paying our last respect to the late 'us'
I should be mourning, but before the horse,
we have put the cart.
Never had you heeded love.
I pressed START off the cuff,
made your ends meet, I guess
I gave in too much.

I was affected a lot.
Too bad it never made the two of us.
How is it so possible that homo sapiens
can be that callous?

I could've seen right through
your iris that you don't need a
man in your life, but a job.
Minerals are what you dug.

I hope you are wealthy now.

I looked further than forth
into it, that my eyes passed the 'breaking up'
heaps unnoticed. I'd actually
blame myself for losing you
only if you never wanted to be lost.
So I blame me not.

Your mission of experiment was
accomplished. Congratulations!
Yeah, don't act shocked, I kinda
saw it coming, I just didn't have
the guts to suck it in. Love is
my weakness and you used it
against me, you said it yourself,
now I'm sure gonna haunt you with literature.

I made it through the clot of
blood that you have put in my heart.
I managed to refract my life
through that aperture.
No no no! Don't get me wrong,
this isn't a grudge, but an overture...

'cause I'm feeling like a material,
kind of a source of an income,
you bet to them we really are,
balls of cells that have no love.

Well, I cannot bulk up hatred anymore,
A stitch in time saves nine.
You said something like, "acting
is my dream job." Now I
see that all times spent with me
were your nights.

I'm trying by all means to use
my low retention as a pesticide
to that parasite.
I've been futuristic with temporary

people like my life was a sci-fi.

No zeugma with our hearts,
I wasn't even counted in your future plans.
In return, I ranked you so high in my
sordit past, holi-crap, solid trash,
the list can't even end.

Being unhappy ain't mean you
gotta treat other people bad.
I mean no one knows what you
have been through until you share.
No excuse for getting others hurt,
this goes to all violent men as well.
It ain't love if it tends to hurt.
It's abuse, so I had to pull the break-pads.
I forgive, yeah, but it's not easy to forget.
Yet I'm over all that you made me
go through, no grudges held.
Just like that!

That was how painful and sombre our break up was!

Chapter E - Eating out with my daughter's Eminent mother.

Waking up at six ante meridiem meant that I had only slept for two hours. Of course, I was still tired, but not too tired to say my morning prayer.

I was a little fresh from the previous night's calls and texts about Basie. I did the math at the back of my mind, while preparing myself for the trip back to Johannesburg. I still had to confront the security guy about my clothes. I still needed to ask Basi how possible could a protected lad had impregnated a girl. I still needed to find a way to protect my fresh relationship from all that drama. I still needed to know how I'll tell my clan. I still -

BZZZ! BZZZ! BZZZ!

I checked my screen, and it was a text from Basie's mother again. It said,

"MrSir, we have to do this the right way. I'll be in Jo'burg today at around two-thirty noon. Can we have lunch together? Yes? No? Maybe? It's on me."

I texted her back, *"Morning Dimamzo (I used to call her that), I received your text last night and I have questions. Well, about lunch, I can only avail myself at Three O'clock. Mind you? Where are we having that lunch?"*

Her response was favorable, *"Nope, I don't mind. 3 will still do, thanks. Let's go to Dro's. The one at Campus Square, Auckland Park - I'll collect you at Braamfontein. Cool?"*

I texted her back, *"I couldn't have preferred it better. 'til then..."*

That was when I stressed myself unnecessarily. In my mind I went like, "WHAT AM I GONNA WEAR?" I searched for the slip I received last time I took items with my credit card, to check if my balance could have still allowed me purchase (on credit) new attire.

I found it and realized that I'd be in short for a pair of shoes. I then disturbed the annuities of my savings account, and lied to myself that I was going to replace it month end.

Had I not left some of my clothes at home the first time I moved to Jozi, I'd have returned nude or with tattered clothes. I managed to buy preferable items and I was convinced that I looked stunning in them.

Had I not been busy before three, relativity would have made the clock look dormant. She collected me where the Mega Bus collected UJ students, and you bet they stared. I wondered why they were going to school on that day (Sunday), but I could only say this in my mind, "Varsity is indeed demanding!"

All they could remark was, "She must be his sugar mama!" ('Sugar Mom' and 'Blesser' were synonymous)

Not that I would blame them, I mean, Basie's mom was quite a catch herself. She was driving Mercedes Benz AMG what-what. I had to be sorry but I wasn't much of cars' fan, so I paid no heed to what type of AMG it was. All I could care about was the fact that it was a Benz! I felt like a significant somebody, collected for a specific mission. You know those spy sci-fi movies...

I acted as formal and determined as possible, as if I was used to the situation. She got out of the car, hugged me in a 'long time, no see' expression, and said, "Wow! You look a-may-zing! Look how grown you are..."

When I was acknowledging the compliment, before I could return it, she had already glanced at her timepiece (Many-Carats-Gold-Watch, you reckon!) and showed me the door in a 'let's get going, we running late' expression, then we made our way to Dro's. She was indeed punctual!

The jam she played in the car - Jazz and Soul music. Yes! She had class and elegance. You'd even think that she was either a business woman or some kind. Tell you what - she was a detective. Yes! She looked moist, 'lady'ish', weak and easy to talk to, but she was considered the most fretted police officer in her hood.

One may ask, "But Mercedes Benz?" Well - I could neither explain nor question her ability to afford her lifestyle, but I could only hope that saying we were in 'South Africa' would explain better. We had a Village Chief as our president, I mean... Yes! That was a nail in the coffin, right? I loved my country, still...

We arrived at Dro's and before we knew it, we had already ordered. After ordering, in my mind, the crazy side of me said, "Dude, you not here for food hau, but to talk! Start already!" I pressed my lips, resisting a smile from that silly thought, and looked at her. I started, "*Dimamzo*, before this starts feeling like a date, I'm gonna compliment you only once *neh*? Then we gonna talk about the issue... You look - you look - young..."

She smiled and said, "Ncaaw! Thank you, aren't you still sweet?" after smiling, she changed her face and instantly looked solemn, then she continued with, "One compliment is enough though. I can now see how you managed to lure my daughter... Now that we are here and you received my texts, do you wish to say anything before I commence?"

Before I could begin - "There you go sir... There yougo ma'am... Enjoy your date," the waitress said.

We just laughed and thanked her, leaving her with whatever she thought. To be honest, I enjoyed the attention that was magnetized by our table. It made me feel like a 'top dog' of that moment.

I began, "*Dimamzo*, I respect you - Big time! We connect - deep! But as for Basi having my child? Naaah! I think it's a trap... I've never - well, how do I put this in a euphemistic way?"

"It's Okay, you are emancipated to be frank. We are both adults here."

"Thanks *Dimamzo*, well, what I'm tryna say is - Basi and I had never indulged in, (sigh) in not using a wrapper, if you get what I'm saying... I can't be the father."

She was a detective indeed! One by persona! She had her way of hearing both sides of the story before laying her cards on the table. I gave her mine. However, hers were unexpected...

She said, "Mhm! You are indeed smart, but my daughter is rather conniving. I do know that you've never went STS (Skin To Skin) with her, but it's not flesh that fertilizes the egg, right?"

"I'm - I'm drawing blank..." my face was dislocated by ambivalence.

"Okay - I'm not gonna beat around the bush. So, I'll just cut to the chase. She said that she 'kind of - sort of - kinda' leaked the wrapper with her teeth the moment she helped you put it on. In my opinion, she was desperate to have your child. She mentioned your genes and stuff - you know Basi and her philosophies -"

"WOW! SHE IS INDEED CONNIVING. But, *Dimamzo* - something doesn't add up - why didn't she tell me the moment she realized that she was pregnant? What took ya'll so long to tell me? Why are you telling me now? Why now *Dimamzo*?"

"You caught her in infidelity, remember? And she was dead to you, remember? After growing up, yet still tenacious - pride and embarrassment deterred her from telling you. Even now, she doesn't want you to be part of her daughter's - your daughter's life. She believes that you'll be a reminder of her childhood howlers and desperation. She said something like - 'her choice then was to rather have your gene than nothing' - believe you me, we tried talking some sense into her for more than two months now, but she always persisted. I had to turn stones and their remnants before I could find your contacts. MrSir, I'm sure you know who we are talking about here. It's Basetsana for crying out loud! Try seeing things from her perspective before rushing into any decision. Surely you'll do what you think is best for all of you. I trust your judgement more than I trust hers."

"*Huuwii*! *Jah neh*? I hear you *Dimamzo*, I really do. I just need to store this away for a while, until enough time passes. When it does, *Dimamzo*, I promise to think about it and sort things out. I appreciate your efforts. Basi might not see it, but she hit the jackpot in the parents-department."

"Still a charmer, I see..." she smiled and shook her head, "and still eating through your nose! What happened to change in this world?" We laughed...

After lightening up the atmosphere with shallow topics which did not require a lot of thinking, I pushed my plate forward as a sign of being through and said, -

"I'm full and content. Thanks for the treat *Dimamzo*! RocoMamas should press charges against you for stealing their loyal customer. Now I have a new favorite restaurant." We laughed... However, in my opinion, they were on the same level of class and taste for my palate.

In a trice, she called the waitress to bring the bill and I was amazed by the aggregate cost. It was FourHundred and Sixty Five Rands, and Ninety Five Cents. But I still kept my composure, acted as though it was nothing.

We hit the road, and in no time, she had already dropped me off at my flat and trailed away back to Hartebeespoort (North West). It was around five post meridiem when I arrived and jumped into my bed. I had temporarily forgotten about the security guy when I passed the admin section.

When I reminisced over everything *Dimamzo* said, I became infuriated. I lost it and turned inept at dealing with the situation to an extent that I impetuously posted about Basi and my daughter on Facebook.

The post went like this:

(It was a picture of a white couple carrying a baby together, and my post was a caption)

"This could be us but you decided
not to tell me until she was Four
months old. On top of that, you still
mutiny over your parent's advice.

Not only hurt will I forever be by the
type of being that you've turned
out to be, but also disappointed
in myself for having assumed that
you were 'smart'!

I've done my part, my best, that is.
I can't take the heat anymore. The
kitchen had just been exited. I'm out
to the mountains of my life to 'peak'
my future and to pick up my faith.
I just need God to do the rest...

I still fail to understand why you
doing this to me. Maybe my level of
comprehension is not that high for
me to be able to understand why
you don't want me to raise my child.
Can a lady, better yet a mother, be that
iniquitous to such an extent that
she denies rights to a father of her
child to see his child?

My flesh is now loose, my energy
is now drained. Not only by studying
and striking for #FeesMustFall, but
also by not being given a chance
to be a better daddy to my OWN and
ONLY daughter. I am not asking for
much, neither am I asking to be part of
YOUR life. I'm not even fighting
for taking her away from you, No! I'm
only beseeching fervently to be part
of my daughter's life.

All I intend to do is to see her, work for her,
spoil her, touch her, hold her, feel my
gene-replica by slithering her skin, kiss
her, tickle her or set her off, ...

Maybe I should stop day dreaming.

It seems like my wish sounds far-fetched
to you, but you bet my intentions are
nothing but tremendous! Now
my dreams about my daughter
are void and mares...¨

After posting, it became so quiet in my room.

Word For The Record: Typically, a lot grow in their father's absence. Their mothers ill speak their fathers, poisoning their children that men are irresponsible. Women can be unscrupulous and callous too, but still blindfold the society with a vision of them being the victims of all predicaments. It's not all single mothers who have been left. There's a very huge difference between 'being left by someone' and 'chasing someone out of your life'.

Chapter F - Formation of partnership in step-parenting.

The tranquility and void in my room stung me with loneliness, and the sting acted as a catalyst to having clear memories of past events. I reminisced over the previous day (The day I went home to facilitate and had a date) and wondered how Blessing would take all that drama. I knew that telling her would sound like asking her to be a stepmother in a two days old relationship.

I knew that she wanted more fun and admiration than drama and frustrations. I was not willing to lose her over anything or anyone. At the same time, I questioned my ability to let bygones be bygones, and it felt a little selfish and childish to have thought that I was not willing to get back with Basi for the sake of our daughter.

BZZZ! BZZZ! BZZZ! BZZZ!

A text from Blessing lightened me up. She was just telling me that she missed me and that she was lucky to have met me. I was a freelancer for any call, so I called her...

"Love'cado," she answered.

"Straw'babe! How beautiful are you tonight?"

"I'm glowing and all thanks to you. You better be handsome there," she insisted.

She had her ways of meeting me half way when it came to romance, yet we were quite different in regard to characters and interests. Let alone the depth in topics. Mind you - we had only met the previous day, had only been communicating for about two months then, yet I fell for her in seconds after seeing her. Touching her was a nail in the coffin for burying my doubts about her.

I responded vaguely, "If it takes that to magnetize you, then you bet I'll be."

"Now I miss you! When am I gonna see you again? Mhm! You'll have to forgive me for not asking you about how your day and trip back to Jozi were. How were they?"

I had been updating her through texts when I departed and when I arrived, but I never mentioned *Dimamzo* and the child yet...

I just couldn't lie. I didn't want to start something so good with secrets and deception. I mean, she had every right to know...

So I rotated my head (with the back of my neck being the pivot) anticlockwise at an angle of hundred and eighty degrees, for a clearer hearing. I trusted my right ear for serious phone calls.

Then I started, "Well - I'm gonna have to start by reminding you something - I... I adore you, big time! I'm intensely fond of you. There'd be nothing more to live for, hadn't I met you. For real - You are the aromat to my bubblegum, the sugar to my eggs, the oil to my custard, the milk to my *magwinya*, French fries to my rice, the beetroot to my Bunny chow... We are that mixed up - quite different, and that's what makes us perfect and strong together. What I ain't, you are. What you ain't, I am. You complete me, and I prefer being with you over everything. Even if it means being with only you in this world, trust me, I surrender all my interests to us being together. I'm saying all this because I'm not choosing anything over you. I'm just including another puzzle to our companionship... My *Belle* - I've just found out that I have a Three-to-Four months old daughter, and -"

"Eh! Whoa! Wait hun - You have what? Mhm! (paused) But you told me that you've never went STS with anyone before *moes? Wabon?* Lies - lies - lies! Men are men, I guess!" She sounded disappointed, down and sad...

"Yeah, Bayb - I've never. She was conceived through a leaked wrapper, pierced by Basi herself! Remember my ex? Basi? I found out about everything today, from her mom. I've never dated such a conniving girl in my life..."

"What if - Babe, do you believe her? I mean, it doesn't sound convenient to me. *Hee!* I just don't want some baby-mama-drama in my life. Mhm!"

"Hehe! Buba! Let's do this neh - ask me three important questions and I'll do likewise. We have to be as blunt and sincere as possible neh? Then we'll use the answers to construct a fair oath. What do you say?"

"Mhm! Baybe, don't go all 'critical' on me hau. I'm only..."

"*OH-Kay*! Then - how about -"

"Nah Baybe, it's fine. We can do it."

"That's my Straw-Babe! I'm gonna ask one, you answer, then you ask and I answer, just like that. Got it?"

"Really bayb? Can't we start already?"

"Okay then... You don't waste time! Do you?"

"BAY-BEE!"

"Okay-Okay! Sorry love... Do you mind raising a child who ain't biologically yours?"

"Eh! Just like that *vele*? Uhm *tjo*! Okay - well - To be honest, I don't mind. What I actually do mind is unfairly being a second priority to you. I may treat her like she's my own, so I'll prioritize her. But you'll have to make sure that she respects me... Now - What would you do if your baby-mama called you in the middle of the night and told you that your daughter won't sleep before hearing your voice?"

"Damn! I'm blessed indeed... Eish - *Jah neh*, the question - *hai-noh*! That would be so dramatic of her! I'd have to reprimand her right away and tell her not to ever act that childish again. Then - turn to you, and apologize for her behavior, as it would turn you off... Now - If I had the last hundred bucks in my name and my daughter got sick, requiring to be taken to the doctor -with a taxi, of course -

while you on the other hand were in short of the exact amount to pay your personal accounts. What would you suggest?"

"*Ao* Babe? I'll tell you to take her to the doc, and probably add my cash onto yours. Then I´ll settle my accounts another time... Love, cradle this into your mind neh: biologically or not, your daughter is my daughter, so I'll have to think like a mother to her..."

"I will do everything in my power to make sure that I don't lose you! Not even an inch of you will be lost..." I was emotional when I said that.

She continued, "*Aah* babe, let's finish this... Now - if her mom poisons her mind and she ends up asking you to choose between her and I. What would you do or who would you choose?"

"One thing for sure - I wouldn't choose. I'll, alternatively, ask her to choose between her heart and her brain. The difficulty in her choice will surely make her understand that I could not choose between you and her. Then explain thoroughly to her that sometimes the concept of 'either' doesn't apply..." I paused, giving her a chance to digest what I had just said.

Word For The Record: In life, there shouldn't be such thing as who comes first. We should weigh matters, not people, according to their importance and people shall be aligned with their contributions and complements. Different people serve different purposes in our lives - learn when to choose and when not to choose.

Then I continued, "...even in algebra, we compare like-terms, and in this case, you and her would be unlike terms. Therefore, you can't be compared and rated against each other. Both of you are of great, yet different, significance in my life..."

"Aaaw Bay-bee! You making me weak now!"

"Sorry love, I'm just saying it like it is... Now, my last question - shall I?"

"Mm-hmm-"

"Do you accept my daughter to be part of our lives?"

"Of course I do, Bayb! I accept her, given that it's not hands ball!"

I giggled a little and remarked, "It could be, plus I don't trust Basi one bit! Now that you mentioned, we'll have to run paternity tests."

"And I'll support you through it all. (sigh) I've never liked someone like this, I even feel thirty! It can't be 'love' yet, can it?"

"You'll never know. It can, it can't. You'll just never know..."

We chuckled and she continued, "Bayb! It´s my last turn *hau* - Where do you see us in the next ten years?"

"WOW! *Jah Neh* - I didn't see that one coming..."

"You mean you don't see us in the future?"

"Nah Baybe, I just never saw the question coming. It's a shortened version of my visions. I expected you to ask about twenty, thirty, fifty - years from now. Ten years is like tomorrow - too close to the present, my love..."

"Oh! So you do see us in the future?"

"Of course, I do Baybe! Who wouldn't when they have someone like you? But let me give that 'ten' a short... In our house, with her and another child of our own, probably owning one car and planning to purchase another one, arguing about which country to visit, probably planning to conceive another child overseas..."

"Mhmmm! Wake up already! Before you get wet dreams..." We laughed.

Then I continued, "My Love'cado-"

"My Straw'babe-"

"Can we make an oath now?"

"An oath?"

"Yeah – that, we shall never break up over anything? That, we shall never let anyone nor allow anything come between us. That, no situation and condition will deter us from being together. That we shall always, and I mean ALL-WAYS, prioritize us, despite who is involved and how much we trust whoever is involved. That - we shall always intend only the good to each other. That - we shall always think and say only the good things about each other and to each other. That we shall make people envy our companionship, and no matter how hard they try to get a piece of it, the love and trust between us would restrict their trials. That - we shall try by all means to meet each other half way. That, we shall involve each other in every decision we make - big or small. That– it willbe 'us' against the world. That ... That we shall be one and inseparable. Can we make that oath? My love…"

She permeated my ear with a cute remark, "Ncaaaw! Bay-Bee! To what do I owe the pleasure of having you in my life *Mara*?"

"Well - To the same Being who gave me the pleasure of having you in my life, and all Praises to Him, huh?"

"Mhm! To Him indeed! Are you ever speechless, though? I mean - Both your eloquence and your ability to think critically and quickly under pressure are tremendous! Good genes for our future kids..."

There was a sudden Cricket-sound silence in my room. Just mentioning genes haunted me with Basie's tendencies. I got worried for a moment. It felt like déjà vu, although I knew that she never had it in her to be able to play cards like Basi.

She continued, "Well - I accept the oath my love. I promise to cradle every line, word and letter of it in my heart."

By the time she responded to the oath, my mind had already traveled to my worries, leaving my concentration hanging around the concept of 'genes for my future kids' in the oblivion of having asked about the oath. I happened to page over from the oath, straight to the concept...

Word For The Record: 'If other ideas run counter to our preconceived thoughts, we tend to 'tune out' the speaker and thus fail to listen.' When you talk to someone and you need their full concentration, make sure if you tap into their memories you give them a chance to reminisce, and also make sure they are back when you continue with your speech. Give people time to think and listen while talking to them - especially if you want them to hear everything you say.

So I remarked, "Sweetness - when are you planning to have them, children?"

"Uhm, when I turn twenty four or twenty five. What about you? I mean - when were you planning to have them?"

"Well - when YOU turn twenty-four... I just wish I had met you before I had exes. I wish you were my first girl. I would've been a few steps ahead in life. But - let me not question God's will and His ways of doing things..."

"My Salt-Cane - now you are hurling my mind into an abyss. Where's all that coming from?"

Tuu-Tuu-Tuu!

'You running out of units' notification alerted me, so I had to curtail my response and hang up.

I replied, "My circumference of attraction, I have to hang up before it cuts us. We'll talk tomorrow,*ayt*? Please continue being this sweet, loving and beautiful..."

"*Ahh! Mara tjo*! I already miss you... Thanks my love, I will, only if you keep your charm and handsomeness."

"You'll have to help me do likewise - Night Sweetness..."

"Nigh-" TUUU! Then it cut us...

My emotions were already starting to get involved and I had to admit that I was 'kind of - sort of' already falling for her.

Word For The Record: Believe it or not, the concept that men are hardcore and callous, that they don't feel and that they are all after 'one thing' ... that concept is a Fallacy! Which type? All of them! It can be a Fallacy of Ad hominem, Irrelevant Appeal to Authority, Circularity, Ambiguity, Straw Man, Irrelevant Appeal to Popular Opinion... All of them! Men have feelings too, most just choose to not show...

I was falling hard for the lady, you bet! The feeling was burning inside me, that I had to express myself to her. I knew well that I wanted to share the poem after few months of knowing her, but my feelings made me impatient.

So I went through the poem I wrote the previous night (after meeting her), edited it 'here and there' and just 'inboxed' it to her, via Facebook, before I slept...

The title of the poem was: *DEEP WITHIN ME*, and it went like this...

A lot nowadays tend to impress
And my aim here is to express
what I feel deep within me.
Neither words can describe
Nor my deeds literally modify
what I feel deep within me.
And this is exactly what I feel
deep within me...

Well - there seems to be a huge possibility
for me to actually not have you in both my
mind and my hands.

As I come closely, slowly but surely,
thinking the trophy is with me,
my instincts disagree with your concerns.

If this sounds like 'just a poem' to you,
well, excuse the impression, for this

is meant to be an expression
of everything felt.

From the very moment we met,
I've let my mind to accept
that I'm emotionally attached
to you - even when I saw no sign
of tit for tat.

I'm a coward, but I can get bellicose
when I tend to lose you.
I just hope I didn't woo too soon.
On the other hand, I thought you
cared less, but as we got closer,
you seemed to oppose my thoughts.

Real Love is all I wanna fall hard in,
that I won't be able to climb back
to the shallow feeling when we fight.
Not 'til I burst my throat will I
stop swallowing my pride.
My heart ain't a liar, now I
wanna stop following my mind.

'cause my aim is not to impress,
but to express what I feel deep within me...

See? I'll neither say there's a reason why
I think I'm falling for you, nor say
there will be why this bond is so covalent,
permanent, way artistic - Donna Claire!

Even Martial Arts, I'll win tournaments
just to certainly have you in my hands.
Your beauty is my ornament,
Brighter than Solar Decks
BWB - Coming with a lack
of stubbornness, how scarce!
You warm my heart that it survives
the habitat of Polar Bears.
Hotter than a fireplace, as I took the chance

to be the poker man.

You give me goosebumps,
in my nostrils, your scent is stuck!
Actually, my eyes are positively phototropic,
and you quite a sun, that hot!

Your complexion lightens up my day,
for us I pray that this ain't
leading us astray,
'cause MrSir Placidfray
is getting settled with you, hey!
I just hope you are here to stay...

Crop the image,
probe the message,
every grain of you that I take
recuperates all my heartaches.
I mean you own all atriums and
ventricles of my heart, down to my veins...

Remember, my aim here is not to impress,
but to express - what I feel deep within me...

Chapter G - Gathering Grounds of the text.

BZZZ! BZZZ! BZZZ! BZZZ!

"Eish! Haah-Yaau-Hamm!" I yawned, wondering what time it was. I chewed the emptiness in my mouth, and swallowed nothing. We all did that when we woke up unready to startle. Didn't we? We would chew like there was a gum in our mouths, as if we had dreamt of food. We sure looked funny, I reckoned.

I checked my screen and realized that it wasn't an alarm, but a text message. I didn't have enough of my sleep, I mean, I had only slept for three hours. It was ten minutes to three ante meridiem. I opened the message box and it was from an unknown number.

It read, *"I'm taking pics with a camera, saving them in a laptop. When I look at them, guess what - damn! I look good in these clothes!"*

I instantaneously caught a headache as I attempted to call the number.

"The subscriber you have dialed does not exi-" then I hung up.

I wasn't too broke to be able to replace the stolen clothes, but I still favored them. I would swagger in them and they would boost my confidence when I strutted into malls and campuses, or at work for that matter. They made me 'me', and the thought of having worked diligently for the cash I used to purchase them, made it a worst case scenario.

I was indeed in South Africa! Not anywhere in South Africa, but at Jo'burg! That reminded me of how I lost my first laptop when I was at Soshanguve (A township next to Mabopane, just outside Pretoria CBD) a year and three months prior to the incident of losing my clothes.

I had movies for days and good music for weeks! My maternal cousin, Vision was her name, wanted to update herself with some of my movies alone at her bedroom, while I was busy with admin work at the dining room.

It was only the five of us at the house - my maternal aunt, her husband (my uncle), their son (his name was Respect and he was thirteen at the time), Vision and I. The house had burglars for all doors and Windows. It was one of those Township Bond houses, afforded and preferred mostly by State-workers or middle class workers...

That evening, I was so busy that I ended up sleeping very late, on the couch, with my laptop in Vision's bedroom. I reckoned that she nodded off in the middle of one of the movies. The following morning, my aunt was the first to wake up. She took a bath and made her way to work. Followed by my uncle, who was collected by 'a friend' and they made their way to church.

I heard only a fraction of their movements around the house - in my sleep - but I was deaf to their conversations until my uncle's departure was accompanied by -

"MrSir, when you startle, wake Respect up as well. You can make anything here for breakfast, but he's allergic to Peanut butter. Just make yourselves at home... I'm out, *neh*?"

Cla-Tj-Tj-Tj-Voom!

As they drove away, I stood up and cleaned the sitting room. I went to Vision's room to wake her up...

"Ko! Ko! Ko!"

I knocked at her bedroom's door, she woke up and told me to go in, and Boom! My laptop was not disposed to my observant small eyes! We thought Respect could have probably taken it, but after waking him up, we realized that he was as blank as we were. We called my aunt and uncle, and they both knew nothing!

We checked if we had left any window open, but they were all closed. Because the house was surrounded by pavement and lawn, checking footprints would have been and seemed illogical. So that was it - just like that!

My one-month old laptop was gone, and it was a dead end...

It was said by the wise that when one door closes, another opens, right? Well - while trying not to leave any stone unturned, ransacking, I happened to receive a call from a school at Mabopane, which required me to facilitate.

Good news was - they offered me a voucher plus my normal charges for compensation. The voucher was worth few hundred bucks above the price of my laptop, at Game. It was just how they worked with all facilitators for gadget access of their goal on keeping up with the Fourth Industrial Revolution (4IR) era. So I saw an opportunity to replace the stolen one.

That day, I had plans with my girlfriend specifically for 'fixing things'. Condolences and I always had silly problems, yet serious on occasions. She was quite obstinate, but always wanted to make things work. She was an insecure con-artist, who was always logical before believing grapevines. She was wild and beautiful, but loose and not quite sane at times.

Losing my laptop swung my mood, and I felt like being indoors until the following day. So I sent her a message, telling her that I had a personal problem that would make me a bad company, so I couldn't see her.

She replied with, "*Please do me a favor neh? Don't contact me unless you wanna talk about seeing me. Losing a laptop can't be a 'personal problem'. You just can't avoid me forever!*"

Eh! I was in no mood for drama. As much as I wondered how she knew about my laptop, I still didn't text her back. The following day I went back to Jo'burg.

All the weekdays at Jozi were just about work and books, books and work, and - work and books. Being too busy wiped the realization that I had last spoken with Condolences when I was at Soshanguve.

Word For The Record: Being too busy helps to avoid brooding over the past. After going through a rough path, don't weep for too long. Just get busy!

She texted me on Thursday noon, saying that she was waiting for me to make an arrangement to meet up.

I replied with, "*Know that the agenda for our next meeting will be: The best way to end things. Matters won't rise...*"

Somehow I felt the necessity to sound formal and a bit legal. My sense of humor still outweighed the seriousness of the situation. However, I was still solemn in my intentions. Levels, right? Well - she texted back...

"*Lol, Ai! Until we see each other, then...*"

I reckoned she thought that I was tied to her, that I'd be nothing without her, that her vindictive clan intimidated me, that I fretted the repercussions of cutting ties with her. Tell you what - I slowly and slowly started caring less and less as she was taking advantage of my ability to let bygones be bygones. She thought she had me wrapped around her finger. *Thol'ukuthi* - hey! (She realized that - hey!) I wised up. I told myself that it was my last attempt of contacting her. I didn't end things, of course, but I just considered myself available for the next rapport.

Word For The Record: Sometimes it is just the 'thought' of being in a relationship that makes us unavailable. I urge you to not THINK that you are in it, but feel. Your availability should be aligned with your feelings, not with your thoughts! However, your mind should also confirm your feelings.

When Saturday came along, the day I met Basie, Condolences called me in the morning with a new number - which I didn't have. I was on my way to Pretoria, when she called...

"MrSir speaking, how may I help you?"

"Mhm - Love - where are you going, today? You sound like you in a car."

"Yeah, I'm heading to Pretoria. How beautiful are you?"

"I wanna be. I'll be in PTA CBD at around ten 'til late. Can we meet?"

"I'm also good, thanks for caring... Of course, we can. It's about time we did this once and for all."

"Skat, you do know that we can't break up, right? We promised each other that we will always let bygones be bygones -"

"I know - well, once is a mistake but twice is a habit. You have too many bad habits that I didn't sign up for. No one can keep up with them. And I've been tryna hope for change, which you ain't putting any efforts to. I'm sorry but - you not the person I fell in love with."

"I am that person! It wasn't easy keeping up with your perfection, but I was trying! Changing wasn't simple - love, especially when you were the only person who was supportive. I have no one besides you. I need you now than ever! Please give me one last chance! You can do anything, but breaking up with me - breaking up with me would be the biggest howler you'll ever make!"

"Are you threatening me now? Watchu tryna say by 'biggest howler'?"

"I love you too much to threaten you. All I'm saying is - don't leave me."

"Word for the record - this is not me leaving you. It's you who's pushing me away."

"Babe, we have come a long way to break up now. You can't expect me to not ruin your life when you ruining mine! You don't know the sacrifices I made to be with you."

"Are you even listening to yourself? Talking about ruining lives and stuff - Eh! You watch movies too much, *wena*! How am I ruining your life? Last time I checked, I improved your life!"

"Babe - You don't understand. Can't we talk about this when I see you? Let's meet at two, Sammy Marks Square, Pretoria CBD?"

"I'll be facilitating at Mabopane within that time interval."

"Okay then, let's meet before you go to Mabopane. Say around ten? I'll take off at Bloed Mall, and we'll walk down to Sammy Marks together. What do you say?"

"Whatever makes you sleep at night!" then I hung up. I had enough of her, tired of her nonsense!

She sent me a follow-up text saying that she couldn't wait to see me. The time I read her text, I was about to disembark, so I didn't attempt to reply.

She - was - nuts! Despite my disdainful responses, she would act like we were still cool, as if it was ingrained in her that no matter what, we would still be together.

I was blind to her temperament until then, and I couldn't help but realize that she was a psycho with a mission in my life. She was not well, neither was she normal. Depending on what you consider 'normal'. She turned alien to how she was when we were still in our early stages of our rapport.

Word For The Record: 'We may all belong to the same species biologically, but socially and culturally we can be so desperate as to seem like different species... No one is right, no one is wrong, but the results can be unfortunate and unpleasant whatever one's precepts,' said Joseph Conrad, in his book, Heart of Darkness.

I loved her - that was what I thought. We dated for only half a year, and during that semester we had already gone through roller coaster moments like we were married and had been together for decades. All the 'downs' were always her fault.

I never caught her cheating, but due to her conning abilities, her smooth talk always helped her get away through confessions. So - I would forgive her, thinking that 'at least she came clean' was cancelling the fact that she cheated. She came clean three times (which meant that she cheated with three blokes) but I didn't even know them and had never seen them. I sometimes thought that it could have been with more, but I couldn't accuse her of anything that I saw no signs of nor had proof on. I even once wrote a poem dedicated to her during our rapport about cheating and coming clean.

The title of the poem was: *Telling The Truth*, and it went like this...

It's all game, I get it...
Pick up artistry - we all heard about it...
I guess we use words to our advantage
Where we should in fact be using actions!

I don't understand why they call it, "coming clean"
when you are in fact "exposing your dirt"!
The main point is - don't go out and cheat,
then come back with "I cheated - I thought it
best to be honest about it."

You don't go out stealing people's properties,
And plead guilty expecting no punishment and justice!
It doesn't work like that!

See? You lost my trust and respect,
The moment you made an act that led
To "I'll be honest about it for forgiveness".

I don't want you to be honest!
I want you to be loyal - to be fair and to
Reciprocate my effort in keeping us afloat.

No phrase can substitute an action, words shouldn't hit home,
Yeah - you can hit me with...

"It's not what you say that matters, but how you say it..."

I know...

However, in this Information Age, the 4IR era -
Hearts react to tangible assets - materials, things that
Satisfy our Four senses, I excluded Hearing on purpose...

Turn to my page - and go home with this....

"It's not what you say that matters, but what you do!"

I repeat, "It's not what you say that matters, but what you do!"

It's time we all came to the realization that -
Words only hit home when they are genuine,
Or at least if they sound genuine - 'cause really,
We won't know - until we read between the lines,

If we heed the lies behind the harmonies of the syllables,
The rhythm of the sentence construction,
and the poetry in word choices...

It's not the justification that counts,
It's what was done.

If you do it - you do it, period!

My response won't be based on the why -
Because I believe we always have a choice of
Not doing it -

A heart is not a logical organ - it won't focus on the
Reasonableness of your actions - it reacts the moment
It receives the message that possess the capacity
To hurt it - and it won't heal until the mind confirms the
Truth behind the message...
If undoubtedly negated...

Pay close attention -

It won't heal until the mind confirms the truth behind the message,

Not the truth behind the reasons why there was an act in the first place!

So don't hit me with, "At least I'm telling you the truth -"

The least and the most part of the whole concern
Is based on "Did you, or did you not, really do it?"

It's not the why and the fact that you'll tell me the truth that will calm me down or make my hackles rise...

Remember, you are obliged to tell the truth,
So don't even dare expect credit on that...

It's the action itself that has the ability to control my reaction!

Acting right and not saying -

Got less impact than -

Acting wrong and not saying!

Acting right is a must - morally, legally and you can add...

But -

Acting wrong is forbidden!

Not telling when you did good is
Not wrong - it won't hurt anyone if they
Found out that you were actually behind
Their success or their happiness -

Even Jesus chose to not answer questions
When He was interrogated by the King
Before ordering a crucification act against Him!

He knew well that He was always acting right,
And there was no point of reasoning -

Hence, reasons are made to lessen - not eliminate -

The impact a wrong act has on recipients!

"Being honest about it"
Is intended to dilute the fact that you did wrong!

Learn the art of doing right by people,
That way - you won't live to justify your actions!

You did wrong, and there's no
"But" or "at least -"
You did wrong, and it ends there!

In that semester, we had approximately twelve 'give me some space' moments and had attempted to break up four times. You reckon it was a crazy and an unhealthy, but an intimate and a promising relationship.

I called it 'tough love', with her having been the one who gave me tough times. We always had disagreements over small and big things. We had frays over almost everything.

She would turn up when I preferred studying. She'd get drunk when I had energy boosters and soft drinks. She'd go like 'In Jesus name' when I went like 'peace unto you'. She would... That was just us, and I was tired of all that!

Word For The Record: As much as differences between partners can be cute and all, it's not all partners whose differences imply that they complete each other. In a relationship, The CHANGE IN happiness gotten from your relationship over the CHANGE IN time spent together will ALWAYS BE NEGATIVE if you continue going for people who do not complete you. You wouldn't want to be in a negative-sloping relationship. Would you?

After taking off at Bloed Mall Street, I met Basie. That was when I decided to just substitute Condolences. I had already cut ties with her in my mind and heart, I only needed to make it verbal, and unfortunately I didn't.

During my first lunch with Basie, I remembered that I had an unfinished business with Condolences. So I texted her, "Something came up. We can't meet. Sorry hey..." Then I put my phone on silence.

The last thing I needed was any disturbance during lunch with Basie. It came to me later that her pride impeded her from texting back, and I considered that my luck. Even after few days, weeks and months, she still never attempted to contact me. Or at least that was what I thought. "Maybe she managed to move on," I could only wonder.

Chapter H - He denied Himself!

Surely the culprit knew me, had my numbers and was having fun. The text gave me a pinprick of apprehension. My nostrils were just too blocked, disabling me to track down the rat that I smelled.

"Which culprit steals and brags about the stolen items to the victim?" I asked myself.

It appeared to me that if I wasn't misinterpreting that text, then the culprit was either crazy or on a psychological mission. He/she was probably not even after my assets, but after me. It even felt right to assume that they could be playing mind games.

Although, it got a little scary the moment I realized that the outcome of the game could be a serious mental, emotional or a physical torture, if not death, I still believed that God had it under control.

I started taking Critical Thinking and Philosophy notes serious so as to solve my personal problems. From then - what I learned at school was no longer just about getting a 'fifty', but about surviving in the real world. I tried to reminisce over any other incident that could help me surmise anything, but nothing visited my skull.

Instead of worrying too much over what wouldn't be deciphered anytime soon, I logged onto Facebook and went through Blessing's Timeline...

Blessing was the girl I made an oath with, the one I called after having lunch with Basie's mom, the one I had a first date with when I was going to facilitate at home...

Yes, that one. Her name was Blessing. I went through her Timeline, checking her videos, posts and pictures, Mhmmm! SHE WAS FLAMES. She managed to rescue my neurons from tearing due to the strain I was under the moment I received that text...

I sure did enjoy every second of going through her Timeline without minding data. She... She was gorgeous! She had... She had a ten out of ten charisma.

She had those T.V Presenter eyes, that business woman nose, those Cosmetic Ambassador lips, that beauty pageant skin, that radio personality voice, that debater posture, that tennis player body, that comedy audience laughter, that public servant heart, that Cat-woman walk, she... She was a belle - my belle!

She wasn't just Blessing by name, but by the impact she had in my life. I was blessed to have had someone of her kind as my partner, and I wouldn't let anything jeopardize what we had. I promised myself that I'd do everything within my reach to keep her...

If luck came by chance, and a chance to be with her was what she gave me, then I had to consider myself lucky.

It was around half past five ante meridiem when I finished going through her Facebook wall. I took a very long early shower, just to wash off all my hardships.

Mondays were known to be blue. Since my weekend was bluer than any Monday could ever be, I planned to protect that Monday from being blue. I couldn't afford to have a long 'blue weekend'.

My plan was to go to campus and just study the whole day to catch up and prepare for my Semester Exams. On my way to campus, I bumped into my paternal cousin. Her flat was just a block away from mine, yet we did not know.

It was on my way to campus and I always passed it without knowing that she stayed there. We never even, by any chance, hit a point of intersection.

That Monday, we had a perfect timing. I guess coincidence could explain that, if not determinism.

She said, "*Aowamfanak'*! Even in varsity your backpack still carries all your books? *Haek*! I surrender! I guess, once a nerd, always a nerd!"

I laughed and responded, "Lee! Is this you? I didn't know you live here - as for my bag, I ain't going to class. I'm heading to the library. I was actually planning to be in campus the whole day. Course is demanding hey..."

Lee was one of the most beautiful, smart and considerate female cousins I had. She was at least four years - but at most seven years - older than me. I didn't know her precise age. What I knew for sure was that her purse was bulky, but her pride was mostly under the influence of gravity. Modest for years!

Her strong affection for 'things' never impeded her from succeeding, and that was one of the reasons why I considered her 'smart'. Well - she was not the type that managed to be in 'top ten' in her whole academic life, but she always managed to get enough results to take her to the next class, next YOS (year of study), next professional and financial level.

Believe you, me, I didn't align brains with academic performance. So according to me, I believed that she was as smart as she thought she was not. Her character of not being penny pinching complemented her eager to explore and travel. She was humble but wild, hasty at having fun but careful and responsible. She was a master in balancing life, I learnt. She was a professional psychologist, indeed.

What she had in mind at any moment would be acted upon at any minute. As long as the petrol tank was full and the purse was flowing with a surplus of banknotes, then nothing would stand in her way.

She was that instant and set to act upon anything that wouldn't contaminate her health and endanger her life. 'Boredom' was just rumor to her...

She replied, "Ask me - I know! Started with Exams already?"

"Nah - not yet - we starting next week."

"Oh - That makes it possible for us to have lunch together *moes*? What time will do for you?"

"Well - my schedule is supple today, anytime will do. What time do you typically have your lunch?"

"Around Eleven and Twelve - you'll hear from me. You haven't changed your digits, right?"

"Sure..."

"You look exhausted though. I hope you don't 'cross night.' If you not careful enough, you'll end up picking up rubbish like some people I know. Next thing you'll be blaming witchcraft - while it's just psychology! These things happen, bruh!"

"It's not books that had been stealing my shut-eye hey - but we'll talk during lunch. Now I gotta bounce..."

"Mhm! You and drama will always be in the same WhatsApp group! I wonder what went down this time. Go and study *mfanak'*, See you during lunch *neh*? Ciao!" She went into her car and drove to work.

Seeing someone in my family, who got me, on that disastrous point of my life, was like a 'breath in, breath out' session just before giving a speech in a full hall. The burden on my shoulders felt subtle, and there was a smell of positive spirit in the atmosphere when I started holding my head high.

If that was how it felt to have just seen her, I wondered how best it would help to have lunch with her. Our fathers were siblings, so that made us close relatives...

Word For The Record: Being shunned by close relatives or important family members can have a huge psychological effect, if not a transient one, in your life. Associates, friends and companions might not fill the void family members leave when they are remote. It is advisable to connect with your clan, regardless of how big your differences are. 'Blood is thicker than water' after all...

I was determined to chow course the whole day, just to tune out from Basie's return. Well - I was determined until I bumped into the 'security guy' right at the entrance of the institution.

I could tell that he recognized me when he glimpsed at me with the corners of his eyes, trying very hard to hide his big round face behind the vacuum space.

I felt the elements of embarrassment and guilt from his facial expressions, and they kind of gave me enough motivation to call him to a halt.

"Mr. ... You'll have to excuse me, but - you look familiar," I said, "have we met before, perhaps? Where I stay? Last week?"

He replied, "You are mistaking me for someone else. I only work in campuses, Sir! If you will excuse me - I am running late..." Then he took off.

"WOW! People were so quick to deny themselves!" I thought to myself. I knew a couple of stories where blokes denied their children, but I knew for sure that an innocent person would never say "I wasn't there" when they actually were.

I also read between the lines, especially where he said, "... I only work in..." and realized that - I never asked him about work. I asked him about seeing him in my flat. You bet he failed to sound innocent! He could've at least asked which flat and which town/city, just to make it sound like he was blank. Did he? Instead, he just went straight to denying, trying not to give me a chance to accuse him of theft.

Disappointed in how inconvenient he was, I let it slide and said, "I guess you are his lookalike. Surely I'll meet him AGAIN. Sorry for wasting your time, SIR." While he was speeding off.

I was bored to the core! The way I was so bored, I even swore to myself that I was not going to entertain that scene in any future citations.

I swiped my student card at the gate, walked into the campus and intermittently glimpsed at him as I trotted past the Central Block. I preferred studying at the Education Campus, for I didn't know many students there. That kind of helped me with maximum concentration and zero-disturbance.

But - on that day I was too lethargic to walk towards the bus stop, which straddled the borders of West and East Campuses, so I surrendered my destination into the Senate House, using the cafeteria door entrance. I took the stairs to the Undergraduate Computer Laboratory.

While I was unpacking my study materials, I noticed a familiar face behind the monitor that was placed horizontally opposite mine.

I stood up, went around the block of computer desks to his, and said, "It was you, right? Were you on protection?"

He was confused and shocked, but knew exactly who I was. He replied, "My *broer*, have we met before? You look familiar."

He didn't look as colored as he sounded. He was stout, dark skinned and his hair wasn't as curly as expected to complement his accent. Well - the accent was a subtraction to my mysteries, but more of an addition to possible deductions. Everything started coming together, converging, until...

"Last year - you and Basie - in my room - does it ring a bell?" I asked.

"*Jy* is MrSir? *Jy's die* same *broer ek* was talking to through Basie's phone? Flip! I'm screwed and used! It can't be *jy*, can it? You? My *broer, Ek* was sent to your room. *Ek... Ek* is sorry *broer, Maar Ek* can't say much. This is my life here! I have to bounce..."

Before I could stop him and ask any question, he had already exited the lab - *real quick*! He was that fast!

I got more and more curious, more and more suspicious and I wondered how he could've possibly not been the father.

"What was he talking about? Who sent him? He was sent to do what? Why? What's happening here?" I asked myself and remained unanswered because he - was - gone!

Based on my character of disliking unnecessary attention, I let him go and didn't attempt to stop nor follow him. I just calmly went back to my desk, unlocked the desktop with my personal student details, went straight to YouTube, and instead of searching for Tutorial and Lecture Videos the way I had planned, I watched a movie. Yes! A movie...

Without realizing that I was wasting time, bulking work, I allowed the plight to conquer my focus. I had too much going on in my life and I had no energy for books anymore, so I used the movie as a pastime while waiting for lunch time with Lee to come along. You reckon it did come along!

Bulking my work, lazing in the lab, allowing problems overpower my academic focus, reminded me of the *Placidfrayan Sonnet* (One of the Sonnets that had my own features, styles of rhymes and construction) that I wrote when I was matriculating, during my final exams. In my high school years, I used to write Sonnets, but I had created my own types...

The title of the poem was: *MY FINALS*, and it went like this...

Ticking towards attention attainment;
Theoretical Optimism approaching banishment;
Full of uncertainties;
Of how many, gotten, will be opportunities.

Heavier than parchment, weighed by mind;
Playfuls, to a halt we grind;
Unnerved, starting with Laws;
O'er glacial brain, Praying for thaws.

With no energy to hold it when it's spitting ink.
Lacking a sleep, eyes making the longest blink.

Highers say, we do halves.
True, no cud for calves.

To reach the crest, 0ne must study.
Procrastination made hardness bulky.

Chapter I - Introspection with an expert.

Lee called me to tell me that she was at the Senate House gate, waiting for me, at precisely eleven-thirty ante meridiem. I had to pack up everything, log out and depress the elevator to the Ground Floor, as quickly as I could. I trotted to her car and found out that we were not supposed to have our lunch at Jo'burg.

I gave it three thoughts and the fourth alerted me that time wasn't on my side. As much as I was tempted to going out with my cousin, to the adventures of exploring the country and letting my palate experience different pleasures, I still had to prioritize 'keeping up with my work' and I did just that.

I knew very well that a stitch in time saved nine. Without sounding like a swot, I told her that I had a group discussion in an hour, so I couldn't afford being outside the city.

She understood - so she thought it best to amicably change her plans. We agreed to have the lunch at McDonald, as it was closer to the campus than all other restaurants and cafeterias.

I got into the car, we drove to McD' and queued for our orders.

We had already indulged in small talks until things started getting serious when she said, "What's best for a child between being raised by her caring mother and being raised by her caring father, when her parents aren't together?"

Bang! It got tense immediately. My eyelids dilated and my eyebrows squeezed. It felt as though she had already and always known my state. She was unpredictable, so I wouldn't know what to assume. However, her profession would be a lead to my speculations. For a moment, a part of me suspected that she could be a clairvoyant. Then - at least - her follow-up statement loosened up my tendons, when she said, "My friend sees it best to raise her child without her father's involvement. Since you are a guy, how would you take this? I mean, if I - for instance - was a guy - I doubt I would go with it..."

I tried to be as calm as possible in my response, "Well - it depends on her reasons. Don't get me wrong, no matter how bad what the guy made her go through was, the child needs both her parents' presence. But - before we judge, we should first relate. It could just be anger and hatred that was talking. Maybe people should start reacting with logic, than with emotions. Otherwise, if the guy wants to be part of the child's life, and he is fit to be near the child, then he has the right to. She can't legally stop him..."

As I was talking, I felt a motion of saliva moving up my throat, as if it was going to be regurgitated. It was an emotional feeling elevating through and up my chest, which was a result of bottling up anger. It had an impact on my voice and made it quite rhetoric that I took that scenario personal.

My response made it sound like I hated her friend; like I was against her choice. No matter how hard I tried to sound neutral, my facial expressions confirmed that something was unease with the topic.

She asked, "Whoa - and then? Why do I get a feeling that you relate? Is this the reason why you never have enough shut-eye *vele*? *Mfanak'* - did you spray a girl? You know you can talk to me..."

Oops! She had me! She connected the dots. I was a little embarrassed and I felt unready to broach the subject; but the bigger ′me′ hurled the smaller ′me′ into the depth of bravery.

I just heard myself saying, "I did, Lee! I did - unintentionally. I was careless to have trusted her, but careful enough to have tried my utmost best to be safe. She leaked the wrapper, Lee! She trapped me - but who cares? It's not my daughter's fault that her mother was deceitful. She deserves to be raised by both her parents, doesn't she?"

She ceased me by remarking, "Wait - you - you have a daughter? And her mom doesn't want you to parent her? The same mom who - trapped you? This doesn't add up! Fetch that tray, *mfanak'*, so we can find a table and break this down. *Shuu-Hae!*"

That time my hackles had risen, and I was the reticent type when it came to my predicaments. I carried the tray as instructed and followed her lead, when she made a signal with her hand to the table. By the time we were both seated, I had already surrendered to opening up...

Because it was McD, she had to collect sauces - when I was settling at the table - before she could join me.

As she was approaching the table, before taking a seat, she said, "You know - I actually saw your posts on Facebook, but - because MrSir is a 'writer', I just saw talent than reality. I thought you were just pulling our legs. Tell me -"

She sat, put her elbow on the table with her hands clasping and continued, "What really happened? Is it Basie? That girl you used to be crazy about? Who is from – Uhm – from hartebees?"

I inhaled a large quantity of mixture of gases aiming at oxygen, sighed, took one huge bite of the drool-drawing burger for energy and explained everything. From the moment Basie leaked the wrapper; contacted me; the incident of losing my clothes; having lunch with her mother; the colored guy's call and his action of taking to his heels at the lab - down to when Basie said that she didn't want me to be part of my daughter's life. I explained and cited just about everything. I guess I needed that - someone to let it all out on - someone to talk to.

I had been bottling things up for too long. It was the best moment to navigate things from a geographical point of view, and the burden became the vanishing points.

She asked, "So you lost your clothes the same morning Basie contacted you?"

"Yeah, the day before I met Blessing, my current girlfriend... Wait - I actually also lost my laptop a week before I met Basie! Something doesn't -"

"You lost your laptop? Where did it happen?"

"It all took place at Soshanguve - my maternal aunt's place - last year, around this time."

"Can I read that text? The one you received today." I gave her my phone and she read it out loud.

Hearing the words helped me link the parts. Especially these parts: "... camera... laptop... these clothes." That was it!

I remembered that I was once mugged in the streets of my main home, M'villa, and I lost my camera that evening...

I was with my paternal female cousin, Mortaz (she was my age), walking in the street that led us to her home. We were about four households away from hers and it was already dark. You bet M'villa was the best developing village when it came to peace and freedom. No one fretted walking at night due to muggers as there had never been any incident of such before.

It was just after exam periods - during the last days of spring. Mortaz was working part-time at a pub called Shine Pub, which was situated next to M'villa High School (the same school I matriculated at), preparing and serving fast food, and selling alcoholic drinks behind the counter.

I went to the pub to check up on her, and we conversed while snacking on French fries until seven post meridiem caught us - which was her knock off time. Mind you - that evening, the pub was open for the whole night for people who wanted to turn up.

As we made our way to her crib, because it was already dark, there was a bridging sound of a pistol behind us, followed by, "Frisk your pockets! I (*funken*) want *errthangya'll* got *witchu* (*ma'funkers*)!"

Mortaz's 'flight mode' was more alert than her 'fight mode' of her reflexes. Due to adrenaline rush, she spontaneously took to her heels so fast that the mugger didn't even attempt to stop her. I was left alone there, stupid and naive enough to have thought that the bloke was pulling our legs.

I didn't take him serious. Home was a developing village, but with no streetlights of some sort. The sun's light was already absent, but the neighborhoods' outside bulbs emitted a fraction of dim light onto the streets. Half a loaf was better than nothing!

Although trees interfered with the light waves emitted, making it difficult to see the bloke well, I at least saw a portion of his appearance - but his face was hidden by a shade of a bough.

Due to less concentration of leaves on those trees, dappled light on his T-shirt helped me notice that he was wearing a beige T-shirt that had indigo stripes.

The pistol was silver and shiny - it reflected some of the light. He held it with one hand and seemed very good at what he did. He sure was a real deal! When I realized that he indeed meant business, because he was swearing and cursing, I only pulled out the camera from my neck and swore to my temporary stubborn head that it was all I was willing to surrender.

When he asked for my wallet, I yelled, "Who takes a wallet with them when walking in these dry streets of this dry place? Come get this gadget and bounce! And when you do bounce, make sure you don't show your face around here again!"

I was pissed, and fretting did not outweigh my anger! I was unfamiliar with being mugged, so I kind of did not know how to react and how to feel. So being pissed was just an optional emotion I obliviously chose.

He just told me to throw it at him. When he squatted down to collect it, I took to my heels - just like that!

Confident that I was quite remote from him, I decelerated to a halt and looked back. It was hilarious to see that he also ran away, diverging from the direction I took. That consoled me. It sort of gave me pride. It made me think that as much as I didn't have a weapon, I was still a threat to him. I felt like a boss! A boss that lost his valuable asset, *ai*!

I remember quite well that... Instead of going home, after being mugged, I collected one of my brave stout looking cousins (whom I related with through the cousin I was checking up on at the pub) to accompany me back to Shine Pub - just to check if the culprit was still in sight - and - he was nowhere to be found...

Word For The Record: After losing a trial - we often look for something to console ourselves with. Be it a small conquer that came as a consolation during a loss or the benefit of losing. We just always try acting as if the outcomes favored us. That is why people hardly accept defeat. They would rather make up excuses for losing and draw your heed towards the schemes and stunts they pulled during the loss. In a nut shell, people don't want to face reality - and it's about time we did! But we can still look at the bright side - every loss has a gain, doesn't it?

... Just after Lee had read the message, I recited that story of losing my camera to her and as I was reciting; I suspected that the person who stole my clothes could've been the same person who mugged me. But - there - was another interesting lead. So I had to continue reminiscing over what happened that evening, and I did!

Chapter J - Justice for an unjust loss.

A s we got into the Pub, an angelic voice stroke my eardrum with a slow remark, "Oops! I'm so sorry -" The source's face of the words froze as we made eye contact.

She was apologizing for stepping on my toe with the hard sole of her sneakers when I attempted to swerve past her.

Because she was FLY, I said, "It is okay, but you owe me."

Her response was collaborative, "Oh! What's the charge?"

It was a new face in my small hood, and it was during my 'game' years. Of course I was not single, but I was just in a long-distance-complicated-relationship with Leticia. I had to open a room for a chaperone to walk me down the 'mourning' lane after losing my valuable asset. It appeared to me years later that she was actually more of compensation!

As it was said in the hood, she was supposed to be a 'ten days' girl.

(A 'ten days' girl/boy was said to be a holiday-visitor whom we would just date for that holiday, and moved on with our lives when they went back to their towns or hoods...)

When she asked, "What's the charge?" I immediately grabbed the opportunity of luring her with both hands - using her guilt of hurting my toe.

I said, "Well, for my toe to heal, it'll take an hour of staring at a beautiful lady smiling or two hours of listening to her laughter. So - which one do you afford?"

"C'mon! Is that supposed to be a pickup line?"

"Nat really! I'm not tryna get to know you or some'ng. You ARE beautiful, yes! But it doesn't mean I'm attracted to you. I just wanna heal my toe - the one you hurt. According to the Law of Conservation of Pain - what hurt you should heal you, mind you?"

She giggled lightly and said, "WOW! You have your ways, don't you?"

"Damn! Did you feel that? I felt the healing process commencing when you laughed. It seems like my hypothesis will be accepted. How about we use that couch?"

"This guy! Okay - I hope you can stand up for yourself, 'cause I have a VERY overprotective and bellicose brother. He'll be here in any minute."

"My hands are good at doing a lot of things but fighting. But - his are quite built for fighting -" I pointed my index finger at my stout cousin (who surely looked like a fighter), then I continued, "after healing, provided that we get time, you might just find out what my hands are good with. Shall we?"

She just smiled and allowed my left hand to give her coccyx a gentle push, while my other hand was showing her the way to the couch.

We swerved and swerved across the drunk, dancing crowd until we managed to lay our 'behinds' on the sofa.

As we sat, she broke the ice, "So - what's it gonna be? You gonna compliment me and I smile? Or you gonna tell me jokes and I laugh?"

Oops! I had almost forgotten that our business concerned my toe's recuperation. I almost thought that I had already won her.

So - for conclusions - I pinched my little charm on her by slithering her cheek with my right thumb, saying, "Princess, beauty is art. It comes in different forms and sends different messages. Beauty can say 'date me', 'kiss me' or 'just get laid with me'. BUT - It can also say 'do all of the mentioned forever with me', or 'for a short duration'. I - on the other hand - am a keeper of what I own, and I prefer keeping my things to myself permanently. So - what's it gonna be? Do we have something in common or - you have the 'short duration' type of beauty?"

Her entire face was numb and in awe of my words! She wasn't even blinking. I saw it best to tweak my speech with an instigation of a soft, slow and gentle kiss.

Her reaction was devoid of resistance as she succumbed to my charm. So - she went with the flow. During the kiss, I patted her neck with my left hand to 'reel' the kiss from being soft and remote to being gently wild and intimate. She could not bear it anymore. She grabbed my hand, breathing heavily, and became herself. She ceased flowing as if she was astonished by how weak she had gotten in such a short duration.

Most of my 'after first kiss' moments were eerie to me - but I didn't want to let that one be. So - I said, "I take it we complement each other. (I sighed) What could stop me from having both your name and your heart? I'm MrSir, by the way..."

"Theee 'MrSir'? Eh! This ain't happening! I'm Condolences. Whatchu doing here?"

"I'm - I'm here to meet you, I guess. Why you asking? What ain't happening?" My face was distorted with confusion.

I wondered if I should've given her the name I received when I was born, if 'MrSir' was too formal and uptight, but I wasn't willing to divulge it yet. I had to be identified as the one and only 'MrSir' just like that!

She said, "C'mon! Surely you didn't know I was gonna be here tonight. Have we met before?" She tested me...

"Nah - I don't remember meeting you - 'cause if I had, we'd be dating by now. I wouldn't have let you slip away."

"Is it you or confidence talking? Or - you are just being a charmer? I heard about you at Sosha, but I've never seen you. Rumor has it that you don't drink nor smoke, so - I didn't expect you here and in a place like this."

"Well - I ain't here to drink nor am I here to smoke. My cousin works here, so -"

"Oh! – Your cousin? And she travels from Pretoria? You know what they say about 'cousins' hey... MrSir, is your girlfriend around?"

"Naaah! Why Pretoria? Where's all that coming from?"

"*Kanti* – you not from*Pitori?* (Pretoria) Aren't you the known 'MrSir' who facilitates at Sosha, Mab-City, - ?"

"Oh - that? Yeah, I do, but I spend most of my time at Jozi - when I'm not at North West. But - this is home hey. It's where I grew up."

"So - You grew up in M'villa? *MoEzweni?* (at a village) As in like - went to school here?"

I smiled before I replied, "Well - I know hey, but you have to believe me. Although I was not born here, I still grew up here, from pre-school until high school."

"WOW!" She was astonished.

I guess it was because of what she heard about me that contradicted my background.

I realized that people from townships undermined villagers. See? I painted quite a different picture of how villagers look, act and sound. Maybe being well spoken was a nail in the coffin!

So - to - redirect the topic, I asked, "Do you, by any chance, dance, sing, model or act?"

"*Ha.a*, but I'm interested in Media. I'm actually an aspiring journalist. Why?"

"It just appeared to me that you have a public appearance... To cut the story short - YOU ARE FLIPPING HOT! I'm not a masochist *neh*, but stepping on my toe earlier actually heated me up instead of hurting me. Trust me - 'it' has never been this hard before."

She got a little shy and reluctantly allowed a chuckle seep out through her nostrils. She probably thought it best to just smile and say no word. Her eyes glinted with hope and jubilation, and her pupil reflected my eager to take things to the next level.

I held her hand up close to my chest, pinned my eyes against hers and said, "Beautiful - I would really love to spend more time with you - and - the units for that time should be measured in years or decades. Now - What can a simple guy like me do to get to the heart of a very beautiful belle like you? I mean, it must be easy for you to get to mine since my chest is this thin."

She smiled and said, "Just give me your numbers - I'll call you whenever I feel like stepping on someone's toe."

I laughed and said, "*Yah neh* - plus you ARE THEEE best 'toe-healer' in the world! Did you go to school for this?"

We just laughed, added more punch-lines, laughed and so on, as I took her phone and dialed my numbers.

It wasn't long after being lost in our fruity physical intimacies and florid topics, when our fantasies were wrenched by a prod on my left shoulder by my 'already gotten drunk' cousin.

He stooped to my right ear, stinking beer as hell, and whispered that he was tired and that he wanted us to go home.

I bid her a goodbye baby-kiss and told her to "please give me that call" as we departed. On our way home, my cousin said, "Yoh Yoh Yoh! *Nikka*! That girl is blazing hoooot bruh! *Nikkas* been tryna woo her and they been failing. But you - my guy - you! You managed! *O skhokho* (You are the man) *mfanak'*! I salute!"

I just laughed and vaguely said, "Game! Son!" I thought that it was alcohol that was talking, so I didn't take him serious - until - the following day, when my friends confirmed that the girl had been rejecting lads for ages.

"I guess I'm lucky," I thought to myself. Even though I knew that 'game' also contributed, I still considered myself lucky...

Apparently, her brother collected her in the morning, and he wasn't pleased with the fact that his little sister spent the night with 'MrSir'. It sounded like he knew me quite well and intensely abhorred me.

The night after that night, she called. During our conversation she quoted her brother, "You can't go around seeing our targets ... You should go for people like us..." and she said that she didn't know where all that came from. It was after two weeks when she became ready to open up.

She told me that her clan was composed of criminals, but she no longer wanted to be part of any of their doings. She 'used' to be a con-artist, and decided to change after we met.

I was too 'drunk in love' to suspect anyone for anything. I just considered myself 'the man' to have had such an impact in her life. I used to tell her that money gotten from wrongful deeds didn't come with pride, but with shame and guilt. That it didn't bring peace but took it. That it never lasted (supporting this idiom: Fast lit, fast gone!) and that to life was morality and to death was deceit. That - blah blah blah! That was just how I met Condolences!

All those sayings about money derived a poem I wrote six months later. Its title was: *Money Is Not A Problem*, and it went like this...

Money Is Not A Problem!

When I say this, people ask if
I'm wealthy or not.

Well - my answer is: I'm alive and healthy!

'Cause the sign next to the amount
in my bank account
is the same sign for my
HIV status - Negative!

Yes, I still manage to say:

Money Is Not A Problem!

I think and solve a lot
while I spend and save less -
'cause my brain is bigger
than my pockets.

I'm a spoilt brat when it comes
to receiving life and needs,
but my Father Above is quite stingy
when it comes to ching-ching and bling.

I dare you to ask about prices and costs!
The answer will always be:
Money Is Not A Problem!

The value of something is mostly
in proportion to its level of scarcity.
Life is more scarce than everything.

One would say,
"Life is just a reproduction away from us."

Another would say,
"Life is just a prayer away from us."

Life is actually a blessing away from us,
and to be blessed is scarce.
So how expensive can life be?

Life feels scarce when you are aware
that it is threatened. That is why
people pray during their tough times.
It is basically due to oblivion that
we don't realize how threatened our
lives are in everyday activities that we
take part in. The true measure of its value
would be explicit if oblivion didn't exist.

Just being alive should reflect a greater
wealth than all economical concepts

of 'wealth'. In fact, living is proof
that Money Is Not A Problem!

Our ancestors survived a barter
economy - so you don't really need
to be rich in order to say:
Money Is Not A Problem!

Money would easily not be a problem if people
were rather purpose-driven than salary-driven.

Did you know that money is not even a factor of production?
It is just a flexible form of exchange.

Therefore, money is not proof that
work had been done, but change is.
It is through fulfilling our purposes
that change can be brought.

Although a paralinguistic greed may
give rise to the duplicity of what needs
are, one would dispute the phrase,
"Money Is Not A Problem."
Because their prevailing knowledge says it is.

My world is not systematic!

What if you also lived in a world
of no exchange, but of giving?
Would Money be a problem to you?

My purpose is to give,
and God gives for free.
So in my world: Money is not a problem

Chapter K - Key to the network.

After reciting everything, Lee asked if I thought my ex girlfriends were connected to the robberies - but I responded not. I was blank and my mind went numb on me. Instead of answering the question, I devoured the burger that had already lost heat and gulped down the soft drink that was close to gaining heat and losing its acid.

The whole 'situation' was draining my energy and I needed as much nutrition as I could consume. I was so ravenous that I ceased eating with my palate, and ate with my villi. Not that I was numb to the delicious taste - I was just prioritizing hunger over pleasure.

"Eh! *Mfanak'*, when did you start digging in like a destitute person now? You are embarrassing me *hau*!" I was oblivious to publicity.

"Eisan! My bad! I'm just hungry hey - it has been years since I had a burger for lunch. Lee - I know you a huge fan of Maxis *neh*? But - have you tried Dro's before?" I asked, trying to instigate a new topic.

She shook her head and said, "*Ha.a* - Where is it? Do they have ribs? You know - I don't take restaurants that ain't got pork serious hey..."

"Mhmmm! Did you change your Church? Or - you one of those?"

"*Mfanak'*, if you read the bible, you'd have read the scripture that says that don't judge so you do not be judged. You don't wanna jeopardize your points in heaven with judgement on sinners,*ankere*? Be a saint and leave us live..." That was Lee for you! What Lee put her mind to, Lee would just make things happen!

She believed that church-goers are mostly hypocrites. She would say that they go to church every weekend just to quench their thirst for attention from their society and from their fellow 'brothers and sisters'.

"They go to church for wrong reasons. People must visit that Holy place for only one reason and that reason is to connect with God. Not to prove a point that you are a churchgoer! We are considered *'bagelogi'* (people who left church) but you bet we could be more connected with God than those 'always present in the House of the Lord' type of people. God favors Faith more than sacrifice. You have faith - you have everything! He exists in us, not in that building. He is our consciousness. He loves us all for who we really are. He identifies us by our real characters and our true selves, not by these church-uniforms, how we greet each other, what we call each other and stuff - *Mfanak'*, you see me - as much as I drink, turn up, hardly go to church and ish, I believe in God. I have faith in Him and I know that I am a sinner. Hypocrites see themselves righteous and I don't. I think that's why I'm blessed. I think the reason why these poor people who always go to church on Sundays without working hard during the week will never be blessed. They live a lie, fooling who?" said Lee.

She spoke a blue streak and I was just nodding like, "you preach! Amen! Hallelujah! Louder! ...!"

We spoke about our other cousins and church, our family structure and its politics, went back to my issue, digressed with how it was to be an elder, back to how I'll tell the family that I have a daughter, and sealed the lunch with the discussion of whether I'll meet up with Basie or not - to talk about my right of being part of my daughter's life - and Lee urged me to make amendments with her and to be friendly with the situation, to take things slow... I took her advice and things started looking smooth.

Hadn't she glanced at her wristwatch, I would've forgotten that I had to go back to Campus for that 'group discussion'.

Peeping at her timepiece was actually my cue to leave - so - we went our separate ways. I felt ready for books, ready to chow course, ready for the whole world! Truly speaking, that lunch helped - big time! It turned branches of problem networks into one single string of a solvable hiccup - especially when I had to consider connecting the dots regarding my lost items, and how to go about Basie's obstinacy. She led me to the key...

I went back to Campus and studied Philosophy - Logic this, Validity that, Fallacies this, Truth Table that, Venn Diagram this, Arguments that, Premise this, Conclusion that... I was flowing, enjoying and understanding. I *chowed* it...

In a trice, which was the precise moment of realizing that I was patched, I was through with the course. As I was closing the tabs on the desktop, after packing all my books and documents, there was a confident voice behind my right ear - that said, "Uhm - Hi, are you done?"

When I looked at the face, I saw a yellowbone! She was appealing and could make any guy drool to fill a mug!

Due to prevailing knowledge and past observations, her accent wasn't clear for anyone of any race or culture, but could be a good lead to assume that she was Xhosa. Her skin was tawny, with a small nose, visible outlines, small barbie lips, white moderate sized eyes - looked somewhere between short and average - had that 'don't approach me' look, and looked focused for decades!

She was one of those 'I know why I'm here' types of students - which would have impeded me from trying my luck on her - hadn't I had Blessing. In fact, she was one of the reasons why I didn't doubt my strong affection for Blessing. She was attractive, but still had nothing on Blessing.

I replied, "I'd be done if you hadn't asked. Now I have to wait 'til you give me your numbers."

"Which numbers? You want my Account-number or my Student-number?" She nailed it!

I squeezed my eyebrows and dropped my jaw in amazement. I had to see her again - I had to know her. I just couldn't date her for I had Blessing and I was content. I asked her which course she was studying - only to find out that we were in the same class. That was an opportunity to network with future associates and I finally saw a study-partner in her.

I took my pen, pulled her arm, wrote my number on her palm and said, "You aren't obliged to contact me - neither are you emancipated to do anything that'll make me owe you. Just use them whenever you feel like having good company."

She was confused. When I read her face - she looked like she would instantly wipe them off and forget that we met. *Thol'ukuthi* (An ambiguous phrase which used to trend through a song - well, here it implied: Then you would realize that...) - she wasn't as 'uptight' as she looked.

"*Haibo*! You - are - quite - confident! Aren't you? I wonder what makes you think I'll use them. Now if you don't mind - can I sit?" she replied.

"It's not confidence hey - it's certainty. In fact, contact me when you start with Algebra - Matrices. I might need your - Uhm - your company." then I smiled while departing.

Due to Doppler Effect, her voice was trailing away when she said, "You not only confident, but proud too!" But I chose to continue walking.

After exiting the Lab, I remembered that I didn't get her name. I thought of going back, and the realization that it would seem like I was after her made me recoil from acting upon my thought.

When I was passing by KFC, ambivalent about whether I should go back to campus, dining hall, to collect my meal or to just buy Streetwise Pap for supper, I received a call from an unknown number. It was a familiar voice, but smoother and softer. I answered, "MrSir speaking, how may I help you?"

"*Haibo*! 'MrSir'? Mhmmm! You really do love yourself, Yoh! What are you doing tonight? Between eight and ten?" she replied.

"Uhm - Can I be cleared on who this is, please? I don't wanna clutch at straws."

"You'll only be cleared if you agree to be at Education Campus at eight. Will you make it on time? Or you have other plans?"

"Wait - is this the beautiful lady I met few minutes ago? You can't be that fast!"

"You call this fast? You must be doing a wrong course or you are simply in a wrong institution!"

I exhaled a subtle chuckle, while responding to her request, "Well - tonight is too soon hey. I'm tired and I was planning to have a shuteye the whole night."

"A shuteye when people are chowing course? We take naps, startle and work, bruh! This guy... Go take a nap and come back at eight. I'll be starting with Algebra tonight."

"Uh-lah-lah! What have I gotten myself into? Am I being punished for giving strangers my numbers? Why can't we just make it tomorrow?"

"Really? Why tomorrow when tonight is possible? MrSir - I work with possibilities and tonight can do for both of us. Tomorrow has its own errands. But - It's cool if you no longer want 'company' - 'cause it's either tonight or never."

"*Eish*! *Jah neh*? How about between ten and twelve? I need to relax and take a *break'nyana*..." I said.

Her response was deep and solemn, "That's COMFORT ZONE! It is what mostly deters us from doing good things. We always want to be comfortable, instead of wanting to be successful. It's about time we started striving towards achieving our desired results and stopped looking for comfortable positions. Instead of sleeping, relaxing or contemplating, we should work, work and just work until we reach our terminus! MrSir - Comfortability should be a prize after winning, not a digression during a trial..."

"Whoa! Are you the same lady I met today? You sound more like an angel than an engineer now - you freaking me out!"

"Ha ha ha! Are you ever serious, MrSir?"

"Serious? Only when I meet normal people - and you aren't even close to being one of them. That was just deep hey - You won. Eight it is - and I hope I won't regret this..."

"You - are - something - else! Just don't be late - I am Punctuality's twin hey..."

"I'm never late for dates. So - I'll convince my mind that it's gonna be one. 'til then..."

"This guy! Bye MrSir..."

"Wait, what's your name? I wanna save your numb-" TUUU! She hung up! She was that fast, you reckon! She didn't even wait for me to say "Bye" too.

Otherwise - Meeting her was a Bonanza! I felt a spirit of positivity in my life. I could feel that she was sent by the Supreme Being. Not to substitute Blessing,of course, nor to be my second companion, but to be my chaperone for my academic journey. I just loved Blessing too much to cheat, or to be tempted. So I considered befriending her...

Speaking of loving my girlfriend, before I took a nap, after eating my early supper (which was at around twenty three minutes past five), I found my mind occupied with Blessing's face. I missed her.

So I took my phone, scrolled down my contact list and changed Blessing's name to 'My Belle'. I was in love!

Because I didn't have enough units for a long call, I thought it best to just text her. So - I selected a 'send a message' option and texted this to her:

"*Knowing that I have you in my life is a source of great solace to me. You bring a deluge of contentment to my heart. You are my niche, the cushion to my fall, the circumference of my attraction... I feel good when I'm with you. You are like my favorite outfit, I look good in you! You are the couch to my toilet, the straw to my main meal, the fork and knife to my drink, the jacket to my summer days, the vest to my winter night, the balance sheet to my Chemistry, the screen to my radio, the periodic table to my L.O... You fill my crannies, you complete me! I really have fallen for you and there's no turning and holding back. My affection for you is in Carats, Joules, Newton's, Dollars, Coulombs and Degrees Centigrade's. It is measured in Giga Units! My Belle, You are mine and I am yours. Enjoy your evening!"*

I then put my phone on silence, set an alarm to wake me up at seven-thirty post meridiem and nodded off.

Chapter L - Lest I got tempted, I Learned.

When I woke up, I made sure that I didn't make her wait for me. I did the 'usual' and saw myself at Education Campus five minutes earlier. As I walked towards the Cafeteria door, something told me to turn around.

When I turned, Boom! There she was - wearing a very short, tight, seductive and explicit dress that divulged both her spotless-tawny thighs and her full-emerged cleavage. Her legs were perfect-shaped and her thighs were full of 'look at me' messages to my eyes. I couldn't resist looking and it was difficult to not lust.

I gritted my teeth, trying to calm my hormones. I wondered which module we would chow that evening: Algebra or L.O - But the latter wasn't optional. Of course Life Orientation wasn't part of my course, but we knew that it was an extra mural activity for most students - either at Res' or in their private accommodations.

She indeed looked voluptuous! I didn't even know whether to compliment her or to focus on our business. I suspected that it was her way of tempting me, of seducing me, until she came to me, hugged me and said, "MrSir - I'm sorry. You'll have to wait for me. I'll be back now-now! I need to change this."

"Oh, Okay! Looking different today - what was the occasion?"

"My roommate and I were taking pictures. So - we had to look stunning *kaloku*."

"*Itjakg*! Girls will always be girls! I don't mind hey - you'll find me in the lab. First floor - room... Uhmm - the second one on your right, it's hardly occupied and it's warmer than others. Cool?"

"Cool!"

"Oh and when you change your attire, please cover everything this time. It's getting cold *outchea* and - I need to focus."

She smiled, glimpsed at me with the corners of her eyes as she walked away and said, "Mm! MrSir! Worry not, I will change. Gimme ten, okay?"

Then she speedily 'cat-walked' to her roommate who was waiting for her in front of their Res's door - which was about twenty metres away from the lab.

I practiced while waiting for her, for about fifteen minutes. She came back wearing a denim jean and a yellow jacket that had three beige sequins arranged in a vertical axis - straddling her breasts - down to her naval. Her long hair served as a beanie for her small head.

I didn't look down to her shoes, as she was moving quite fast while talking, when she was approaching me. She just looked proper that time around!

She apologized again and asked if I had mastered any chapter in Algebra.

I said, "Pride aside - I'm blank hey."

"You must be kidding me!"

I learnt from an eminent mother of mine that it was ´not cool´ to praise myself. She always told me that it was better to be praised by those who found me praise-worthy than being boastful. I had to prioritize learning over being respected.

So I said, "For real hey, but I remember a thing or two from lectures. The rest - I scanned them when I was still waiting for you. Just don't test me, please. It's clear that you the smart one here. So - do we - start with Tuts or past papers?"

"No one is smarter than another in this institution hey. We all qualified for this course. Please never doubt your intelligence again in your life!"

"Ncaaaw - that's so sweet. You look cute when you motivate someone. Just look at yourself!"

"Mxm! *Wena* you never take things serious!"

"Sorry - Just that you take me too serious. Anyhow - Can we start? What are we gonna start with?"

"You see me - me when I practice math, I always go for YouTube videos first. They help me understand the concept better, and they offer exam type questions as examples. *Futhi* they offer help from respected professors from highly ranked Institutions such as Harvard, Oxford, you name them... If they work for me, then they can definitely work for you, MrSir."

"That's cool - but be careful of using conditional arguments hey. You know how Logic works. 'If - then' isn't a light phrase to propose."

"C'mon - MrSir! Philosophy is just a module to me - not a way to live. Cut me some slack, *hao*!"

"I'm sorry - I never thought you'd dislike such a heavenly-sent module. So much for being a Christian! However, this is something disappointing about us, students. We don't study for application and knowledge. We study for passing. Don't you think Philosophy is significant for your career?"

"If it is - then I'll revise again when I get a job. That's if I'll get a job, 'cause *hai* - with the current unemployment rate, one would never know. So I just want a degree and I'll cross the bridge when I reach it. Being too futuristic is also absurd in philosophy, or *kanjani*?"

We laughed. I interfered our laughter with, "So are you gonna watch the videos for - like - ten minutes or -?"

"Well - the duration will be contingent on the complexity of the chapter. Which chapter are we starting with?"

"I can do with any chapter hey. When you watch the videos I'll be treating past papers. Just gimme a nudge when you done, *ayt*?"

"Whoa - MrSir - Why do I get the feeling that you wanna cram? Or - you already through with the concepts?"

When I said that I was quite numerate when it came to Algebra, she pleaded for a summarized explanation and I delivered. As I was explaining, I learned even more myself. I also realized that I enjoyed breaking down the concept for someone else more than I enjoyed studying to pass. I felt like explaining the whole night - passing my knowledge on. I was going deep, thorough and I was clear with every syllable. Because she was a fast learner, she grasped real quick. The thorough I went, the more I learned myself...

Word For The Record: 'If you can't explain it, then you don't understand it yourself.' – Albert Einstein said. It is not simple until you can break it down. The benefits of sharing knowledge are figurative - you get to master it even more. In order to understand more - you have to explain it better. Just find someone to explain it to, or use that person in the mirror!

After explaining, certain that we both got the concept, we started treating past papers, perusing, deciphering most of them, and we also mastered all subtopics of Matrices.

Time flew and in a nick of it my phone vibrated. It was a message from Blessing. The vibration reminded me that the last rotating bus that headed to the Main Campus would be there in less than twenty minutes. I prepared for my departure during the interlude between studying and reading the text message.

The message read as follows, "*I frisked all my organs for my heart, and it didn't take me to become a sleuth to realize that you are the one who stole it. I hope you gonna take care of it! I'm more involved with you than you are with me - goodnight Buba...*"

I read it slowly in my heart, smiling, as I planned to leave.

"Haa! Are you blushing MrSir? I wonder who sent the message that got that kinda effect on you. Is it anyone in campus?"

"I ain't blushing - wait, I still haven't gotten your name. According to how our first session went, I strongly believe that I'm gonna see you again or more often. A lad needs to use your name in his future references hey... Do you even have one?" I had to change the topic...

"Mhm! You and words come a long way huh? But - like - on a serious note though - who doesn't have a name?"

"Jacky Chan on *Who Am I*?" then I grinned. I knew it was a lousy joke but I hurled it anyway.

She told me her name when she was giving me a 'goodbye hug' before I got into the bus. Her name was Nosipho. It confirmed my assumption, based on her accent, that she was indeed Xhosa.

The idea that Xhosa ladies were expensive was a bit of a cult in my country, and it was what made me give a wide berth to them. I knew for sure that I wouldn't afford meeting their demands. Nosipho didn't quite seem and sound like an exception, but I could only hope that befriending her would either be cheap or free. It was instilled in me that no beauty of a Xhosa woman would draw me. Instead, I chose to use her discipline for my frivolity. Our first session was a pragmatic approach which declared my choice the best! (Was I guilty of stereotype? I was only human!)

The boredom in the bus made me call Basie. I didn't know why, but I still called her. When she answered, I didn't know where to start. I had to clutch at straws, ad libbing my reasons for calling.

"Hi, Uhm - long time hey - I - I hope you good. Are you home or at PTA? I - I would like us to meet," I spoke before she greeted me.

"I'm - doing great, thanks. I hope the same for you. Well - I'm in Jo'burg, Mayfair. Do you know the place?"

"I think I do. You mean the one that is mostly occupied by Indians, behind Brixton, Auckland Park, from Campus Square?"

"Yeah - I'll be here for two weeks. Are you also in Jo'burg?"

"Yeah, can we meet at Brixton Shopping Centre? Jeppa Duo Restaurant? Or you don't mind coming to Braam? We'll use Wimpy."

"Wait - why?"

"I don't know - honestly. We'll both know if we meet. I guess we need closure. It really irks me that I'm not on 'speaking terms' with the mother of my daughter..."

"MrSir, I really don't think it's a good idea to reconnect. Your return will complicate my life. It's gonna be weird. What I did to you ain't worth forgiving. Unless you on some 'revenge-seeking' tip - of which I won't allow. Actually - who said she's your daughter?"

"Caamaaan! Basie! You wanna tell me that you didn't know that I had lunch with your mom yesterday? Well - she explained just about everything - from how we conceived our daughter, to why you chose not to tell me. Look neh - I don't want us to reminisce over what happened. All I'm asking for is to have lunch with you. I want us to... Let's just have lunch tomorrow - please!"

She sighed, tuned out for few seconds and said, "Okay! Let me sleep on it. I'll text you in the morning. Good night MrSir!"

"Have a halcyon one, Basie!"

It wasn't long after hanging up when the bus reached its terminus - Main Campus - so everyone disembarked.

It was dark and cold - not 'as hell,' of course - as a winter night. The breeze that collided with my face had no heat at all. The air particles accompanied by the breeze instantly sucked the heat out of my skin, leaving my body with difficulty of naturally replacing the energy lost.

It was around half past ten post meridiem - and the only restaurant that was still open was McDonald. I had to flounce to it as quickly as I could for a Styrofoam cup of coffee to shame that weather. You reckon if it had human qualities, it would have indeed been shamed! Coffee never disappointed me. So - I sipped it 'til I arrived at my flat.

As soon as I jumped into my bed, I tried to call Blessing, but it appeared to me that she either had already slept or had been busy, with her phone remote from her. So - I pulled back my attempt of reaching out and found myself missing her big time!

I placed my pillow in such a way that it was leaning against the wall - with its face perpendicular to the mattress, - took my poetry journal, my pen and the sundry, sat with my coccyx, my upper back leaning against the face of the pillow, folded my legs, placed my journal on my left thigh, sighed for inspiration and energy, then wrote, wrote, wrote and wrote! I wrote until I was lulled to sleep by the luscious metaphors of my own writing.

The title of the poem was: *Now You Understand,* and it went like this...

We started with a big bang
Everything happened so fast
Giving rise to the remnants of uncertainties
And inclining the acceleration of your reluctance.

I felt like you were pinching a quarter
Out of your bond-sack
Yet your disposal left me content
Even when you tried to hold back
Your presence more or less
Divulged your whole bag.

I wish my deeds would express
A high electronegativity on you
So you can spend the majority
Of your time close to the nucleus of my life.

Study you to a point where I'll no longer
Ask questions like - how do you feel?
What do you want? You know -
Graduate with a PhD in Knowing You.

Gaze at you - make sure
that my iris gets a motionless spot
On my eye ball.

Dilate my eyelids so that no blink or eyelash
Can disturb the view.

You bet my optics come in GigaPixels, clear!
To a point where every element in air particles
Will diverge, creating a path for your beauty
To be captured in my brain,
Without any destructive interference.

NOW YOU UNDERSTAND when I say:

You are beautiful...

I heed every word you say,
Understand every point you make,
Note every message you pass,
Answer every question you ask.

When you speak, when you speak,
Before your lips could repel,
My ears are always ready to receive
The melodious waves of your voice.

Even the wax and hair that shade my tympanum
Splits up, parading the message of your royal sound
Through the inner pillar messengers -
Hammer, Anvil and Stirrup.
Poetically applauding and praising
Every syllable said - flowing onto the
Red carpet of my cochlea,
to be crowned by King: Organ of Corti.......

Your Highness -

NOW YOU UNDERSTAND when I say:

Your demand is my command.

Tickle your palms
Biting your lips
Compress your shoulders

Slithering every surface area of your skin.

When I touch your skin, when I touch your skin
The tips of my hands prod my sensory neurons
Into telling the spine to not send the messages
To the motor neuron - 'cause this time around
The aim is not to arouse.

But to share the Valence Electrons of every
Building Atom of our flesh.
Covalently bond, chemically react
'til the composition of our emotions
Change from sad and lonely
To Jubilant and committed.

Press my palms and arms against your back
Pulling you towards my chest
Maximizing the level of closeness
'til we look like a pair
Of diatonic molecules.

Squeeze you so tight for a long time
'til we confuse mitosis into developing
New cells that will accommodate
Permanent attachments like those
Found between conjoined twins.

Highly concentrated with every bit
Of you like a container of fusion
But never up for dilution.

NOW YOU UNDERSTAND when I say:

We are one....

You just never understood how deeply
Involved I am, did you?

But hey - with all being said, I hope -

Now You Understand!

Writing the poem reminded me of one of the short poems I wrote when I was still a teenager, dedicated to Leticia at the time of writing. However, the inspiration behind the poem was prodded by another poet, whom I got the title from. Leticia was my high school girlfriend...

The title of the poem was: *The Gentle Girl*, and it went like this...

Talking about a girl of good social position.
Whose deeds show a perfect ignition.
With a very warm heart that
can melt any glacial action.
Her smile dominates all
other facial expressions.

Only sweet words come out of her mouth,
like a lyrical exhalation.
She heals hearts, her presence
brings about recuperation.
For her absence, there is no substitution.
From Kinetic emotions -
To Potential - she is the conversion.

WOW! She brings an existence
of a joyous interjection!
Her reflection shows an excursion
of indirect proportions
compared to any of her living conditions
leading to an explosion of her inner beauty's vision.

She lives to be gentle, vocation.
Add new human qualities, injection.
She is the gentle girl I can give
all my love to, with no limitations.
For both of us, with Heaven, we shall
experience inelastic collision!

Chapter M - 'Meet' the Mother of My daughter.

"Damn - dawg! Wake up! You wrote new poems and you ain't told a *nikka*? Ammo gotta see 'em! They dope and deep bro - are you in love?" asked Toni.

I opened one eye, struggling to detach the eyelids of my other eye due to the sleep dust (dried Rheum) of the night. His face was blurry, but I could partly see that he had my poetry journal in his hands.

I replied, "*Hoa-hummm*! (yawning) Nikka! What time is it?"

Then I frisked my bed, while slowly getting off it, searching for my phone. It took me few seconds to finally startle and I remembered that Basie had to contact me for a confirmation of our lunch. I also wished I could call Blessing before she went to school.

It was awakening to see that Eight-twenty ante meridiem was accompanied by seven missed calls and eight messages. I asked Toni for my poetry book, telling him that I was late and that we would talk about art when I returned.

He replied with, "We must work on something fresh dawg! I'm performing tomorrow night - you should be on the program."

I nodded as I quickly took my toiletry bag, my towel - while putting my slip-slops on - and made my way to the shower.

I checked my messages when I was fresh. Only two of them were text messages, and the rest were PCMs from numbers I didn't have on my contact list.

The first message was from Basie and it said, "*Morning MrSir, let's rather meet at Burger King Restaurant - the one just outside Gautrain Terminus, Jo'burg Park. I have a trip to Rosebank - so we can meet at least an hour before I embark on my journey. Yes? No? Maybe? Say around one post meridiem?*"

The second one was from Nosipho and it said, "*Hi MrSir, I hope you went back to your room safely last night. Studying with you was really productive. Now I chowed my spot tests past papers. We should meet again today. I'll be studying Computational engineering at around two. Let's meet where we first met - if you'll be available, of course.*"

Among the missed calls, three of them were from Blessing, two from Nosipho, one from Lee and the other one was from my maternal uncle - named Preach.

I wondered why he tried calling me that early, so I made an attempt to call him back.

"You have reached your call limit, please recharge..."

Eh! I checked my balance - Oops! Triple Zero!

"But... how?" I asked myself.

It was later when I was on my way to Park Station when I realized that I slept with my mobile data on.

Apparently, South Point Student Accommodation Officers gave us(tenants) Five Giga Bytes of data per Semester, but mine had already been depleted. I didn't notice that it was running out until it led to the depletion of my airtime!

Gautrain Park Station was a six-minutes-walking distance away from my building, and the main campus was about two-third longer in the opposite direction, from my flat. That implied that I would walk for about sixteen minutes from campus to Park Station.

I had to go to campus to study (since I was behind) then knock off at around twelve-thirty for my lunch with Basie. I did just that...

I arrived at Burger King when it was ten minutes to one, with seven people queuing to order, so I had to stake a spot. She arrived when there were only two people in front of me.

She pressed my shoulders with her soft hands from behind, with her face on my right ear, and whispered.

"We can go to Hungry Lion, if you mind this one - it might strike some memories hey," she said, "how long have you been here?"

"Less - than - ten minutes..." I turned, paused, gazed at her, dropped my jaw, rearranged my face with a 'thinking' expression and said, "Damn! Aren't you still fly! Well - Hungry Lion would mean more than 'just lunch' you reckon." Then we smiled.

I wasn't sure if being nice, being gentle, and the sundry, would complicate things, or would just ease the tension that had long existed between us. However, that lunch was mainly for my daughter's sake. Nothing more - nothing less!

So - she greeted me with an intimate hug, but my coordination was chaste. It was after hugging me, when she saw it best to respond to my compliment.

So - she said, "I have to look good if I have to compete with them ladies I see eyeing you. I mean - I'm a beautiful mother to a beautiful daughter of a handsome father. You haven't lost your touch yourself! Long time, MrSir! How have you been?"

"Bad! Trust me - very bad! I'm incomplete *outchea* - and..."

"Whoa! Not so fast, MrSir! Can't we order first? Yes? No? Maybe?"

"Food! Yeah - food! Eish! My bad Basie, I'm just taken - a bloke had been waiting for that question hey, food!"

After ordering, we silently waited for our orders. I would constantly glimpse at my wristwatch whenever I turned nervous, or check my phone's screen. Few seconds before our tray of Burgers would make its way to our busy faces, she asked, "Have you turned shy now? Or – you are just quiet? You are more of a man now than you were when I last saw you. But - I prefer the 'boy' side of you..."

"Oh - Kay -"

"Yeah - what happened to you? You are too stiff, *mahn*! Are you somehow too 'grown' to be loose? Or...?"

That was Basie for you! I expected her to be more grown than I seemed. I expected a solemn mom with declined sense of humor - like a chicken that had just laid an egg. I expected her to be composed and uptight. Not Basie! Neither a plight nor a predicament would restrict Basie from being jolly and alive. Not even having a child changed her...

It felt different and awakening to start our lunch like that - with that energy. Not that I preferred it that way, but it was better than how it would've turned out - had I been the one to lead it. I didn't respond to her questions. I just collected the tray and told her to pour us soda.

Burger King had that ´help yourself, with drinks (Pepsi), however and for free´ vibe that made the restaurant look and feel quite international – like we were at America.

However, all smart people knew that, according to Economics, there was no such thing as ´free´ - somebody had to pay...

We sat, dug in like we were already full and she broke the ice with, "MrSir, you look tense. I'm trying by all means to make this as smooth as possible - but - you not meeting me halfway. Do you regret this?"

"Naaah - not in a million years will I regret anything. Thing is - you have grown hey - kinda developed. You've turned out looking, sounding and acting the way I've always hoped you would. It's more like -"

"MrSir - everyone gotta grow at some point. You just have an old soul - that's why I couldn't keep up with your growth-rate. We are parents now and -"

"Wait - did you just say 'we'? I thought you never considered me her father."

"I thought I was 'dead' to you, either! Things change, people grow and life goes on. We just have to learn how to ´never say NEVER´."

"Eh! And then - who are you? What did you do to Basie?"

She giggled with a heavy chuckle that you'd mistake with a sigh. It sounded like she was trying to hold it back, preparing herself for a long talk of surprise. You'd gamble it was worth the preparation!

Although a part of me thought things wouldn't easily go well - the turn of events was still beyond my expectations. I was ready for peculiar things to happen, but Basie went over the peak. I saw nothing coming!

I said, "So - this means that we gonna raise her together? You allow me to see her?"

"It depends."

"On?"

"Your relationship status - and - how serious you are."

"I'm drawing blank now - what if I'm single?"

"Then there won't be anything that'll deter us from raising her together - and - by 'together' I mean we might just fix things. You are a good bloke, MrSir, and I -"

"Yeah – Sure… A good bloke you took advantage of. Basie please, let's not talk about us, but her. I'm not here for -"

"Yoh! Clearly you haven't forgiven me. Life can't go on for some people, after all. Tell me MrSir, how will you father a child if you haven't forgiven her mother?"

"I forgave you - a while back hey. I just don't see 'us' anymore. Basie, you one of the most beautiful women I've ever seen. A lotta guys must be drooling over you, queuing for an opportunity to be witchu. Why would you still be after me? Why can't you move on?"

"MrSir, it's about time you've been frank wimme. There's someone else, isn't there?"

"Wait! Did you say, 'else'? She can't be 'else' if she's the only one, right? Well - FYI, there is someone and I-"

"Do you love her?"

"We've been together for a week now, but I've already falle..." my answer was interrupted by a preceding command.

"Ah! It's new love? Dump her!"

"Excuse me?"

"Yeah - dump her. You wanna be part of your daughter's life, right? So you'll have to dump her."

"I don't understand."

"The only way you can be a father to my daughter is through being with her mom. MrSir, you've loved me before. It can't be that hard to love me again..."

"Basie - are you aware that you are blackmailing me here? Do you realize that the Law is on my side? You are in no position to give me terms! You aren't a saint here, and I -"

Her phone vibrated and after checking it, she said, "Thanks for the lovely lunch MrSir. This is my cue to leave. You'll tell me how 'hurt' she was after dumping her, *ankere*? But I bet she won't hurt - she's not as involved witchu as I am. Actually - No one will ever be, but me. I'll call you -"

She spoke while grabbing her handbag, giving me a chaste kiss on my left cheek and making her way to Gautrain Park, without giving me a chance to say one more word. Neither a chance to ask about the colored guy nor a chance to ask about the incidents of losing my items, were given to me. She left me hanging...

I was left in awe - not believing my eyes and ears. I even tried to put myself in her position, and I realized that it was logical for her to assume that she meant well, as a mother, because it was not easy for her to forget about me when she had my daughter as a reminder of what we had. It came to me that the more she bonded with our daughter - the more she inevitably and obliviously bonded with me.

It always seemed easy to dump a girl whom you have just met few days ago - but Blessing was a different story. Basie had to forgive me! Yes, it would also be sweet and romantic to be with the mother of my daughter, but I saw myself with Blessing in the 'future'.

Basie had it all that I had, Blessing was all of what I wasn't. Basie was a female version of me, but Blessing was the missing part of me. Basie was already a woman, she was old and she was a mother. Not just a mother, but a mother of my daughter.

Blessing was still young and wild. She was younger than me - a year more than half a decade younger than me. But - they were both beautiful - equally beautiful. They both met all my physical requirements. They both respected me. I was confused.

Of course, I knew Basie more than the way I knew Blessing, but I had to give Blessing a chance to know her better. Basie was deep and critical; Blessing was wild and shallow. Basie was talkative; Blessing was a good listener. Basie was manipulative; Blessing minded her own business. Basie was a writer; she was thorough and articulate when reciting a story. Blessing would just summarize and point out only the interesting parts...

Although Basie had a child with me, knew me well, she still couldn't wipe Blessing's existence in my life.

Having a child with Basie was not enough to eradicate the bond that had already started to exist between Blessing and I. With all my heart, I chose not to leave Blessing. I chose not to dump her!

Stuck on my table, eating through my nose alone, I eventually lost appetite. The lunch was too much for an over thinking lad. Basie indeed left a Bomb!

The comparisons I made in my mind made it difficult for me to decide. My mind failed to be convenient to my heart. So - the obstinate part of me said, "I won't leave Blessing, no matter what!"

My meal was barely half eaten, but ego and pride didn't allow me to ask for a doggy bag. So I left them there and flounced back to the campus.

On my way, the Christian side of me intrinsically had a conflict with the infuriated logical side of me. It was a matter of 'take her to court' versus 'let God deal with her stubborn heart.'

By the time I arrived into the Campus, it was already well with my soul. The 'Faith' side of me won...

That brought a poem later, about the Supreme Being. The title of the poem was: *Stick By Me*, and it went like this...

Something big attracted my receptors,
And before I knew it - it was God!
He just WAVED,
And out of IMPULSE,
I shrieked, it was Love at first sight,
Chaperoning down my nerves,
It was made clear
That I'm sensitive to change,

He sensed it...

He said this:

"Don't you worry, I have no use for your Sensory Neurons,
My child, I'm after your immune system.
I'm here to heal you - I'm after your Spine,
I wanna move you! I'm after your Digestion,
I want to feed you -

Don't just feel Me, receive Me with your being,
I'm not here for your receptors, I'm here for your
Life!

Your flesh is too small for My Breadth and Depth,
I'm extra large - so don't just open your arms,
Open your heart!"

I was like - OMG! This old Man is good
With words hey -
I mean, He created them - so I had
To give Him that...

And He continued...

"Stick by Me, even when things don't go well,

Don't lose a sight of Me,
Focus like a Hitman,
Aim at my presence,
Pull your openness -
Shoot all your spiritual problems at Me -
Just make Me your target!

Stick by Me...

I will shape your faith like a personal trainer,

Stick by Me, ...

I will serve your soul like a restaurant waiter,

Just stick by me!"

Hehehe y'all have no idea of how big my God is...

You hear them say, 'what goes around, comes around,
Money makes the world go round, blah blah blah,'
Who do you think is the Pivot?

Even to those who wanna smoke weed to forget
Their miseries, those with low self esteems -
To feel high and look fly -
Guess who will be the Pilot!

Yeah - that's my God for you...
He continued...

"Don't kneel and pray about your earthly problems!
Thank me for trusting you with them!

Don't cry to me and ask for my help!
Don't sit back and wait for miracles,
Don't even expect them!

You are in charge of the earth!

My son - everything about life is a miracle,
What more do you want?
Should I break it down?"

To be honest I was a bit confused,
Doubt and anger got me consumed,
Before I got dramatic like Tom Cruise,
He hit me with a pang of Conclusion...
He continued...

"I made a man in My image, and made a woman
Out of a rib of a man - what does that say?

I repeat: I made a man in My Image and extracted
A woman from the Man's rib -

What does that mean?"

I tried to break it down -

If God doesn't have both genders, then a woman
Is not a gender, she is part of man - part of God!
If a rib is meant to protect one's heart -
Then we as men are weak without women!

Simply because we are one with them -

Women are our feminine sides -
And God has both sides around Him.

The Story Of MrSir (Word For The Record)
Page 116

That is why marriage is a prerequisite for Pastors.

They need to be complete before they can preach!

My hair swirled like cooked noodles from
The burning of my brain - my head was like
A bowl of pasta -

I received spiritual wisdom, knowledge and understanding!

Women and men should appreciate each other's
Existence as being one to complete the flesh
Version of God! Gender does not exist!

God is love - and marriage is the best version of God!
How do I then stick by God when I don't respect
The flesh version of His rib?

I see! More reason for men to love women!
And women to respect us in return -
Ribs are protectors of our hearts so that we
Can love without fear!

And protectors are meant to respect their Masters!
Makes even more sense now,

but God had ...

To put a nail in the coffin,
He blessed my analysis with,

"When I say Stick By Me -

I don't mean,

You should relax and depend on me with what
Your five senses can perceive and interpret!

You are the earthly version of me -

You can do what I did when I came in Flesh (Jesus) -
You are blessed with an ability to solve your own problems -
I'm only here for your spiritual battles!
Everything else is contingent on your own faith...

Pray - do - and keep on repeating the cycle -

The cycle is what will strengthen you -
It will help make sure that what you build and pin sticks!

My child - for your deeds to stick on earth -
You have to Stick By Me!

Women respect Me - and for you to earn their respect,
You have to Stick By Me!"

Without going around a circle, I stopped
At a point so blank that the tangent got
Straight with His ratio of changes:

The gradient was: Stick By Me!

Chapter N - Networking and its *Coincidences*.

I was astonished to find Nosipho half way through with Computational Engineering. When I checked my timepiece, it was already quarter to three post meridiem. Basically, I was forty five minutes late. I trotted a little towards a row that had one empty chair and staked it out with my backpack, then went to her. Due to not wanting to share my personal matters with her, I popped with a distracting theme so as to isolate her focus from my lateness.

I moved closer to her chair, stooped to her left ear and susurrated, "Nosi, after getting laid with your bloke, who wakes up first?" She was filled with the emotional impact of overwhelming shock.

Her response was rather high in pitch and attention-drawing than composed. She remarked, "Did you just say 'getting laid'? *Haiboo*! I'm still innocent, MrSir!"

Then everyone in the laboratory sandwiched us with a deluge of heed from all dimensions. I had to admit that I was a bit embarrassed. I knew for sure that they all thought I was trying my luck on her, which they probably suspected that it was a flopping luck, but I calmly countered, "Poor guy! How long have you been with him?"

My calmness affected the tone of her response. She replied in a low pitch, as if she also felt the pressure from the attention she had drawn with her previous response, "I've been single for about three months now. Why are you asking? You - you are naughty - you!" She pointed at my nose with her index finger, smirking. My mission was accomplished. I reeled her heed away from complaining about my lateness to being curious about my 'out of the blue' question. I was done!

Continuing with the topic would have made me look cunning, so I didn't answer the question. Instead, I just asked, "Done with Spreadsheets?"

"I can't say I'm done until I treat past papers. I treated lab questions though, and so far so good. How confident are you with Comp' Eng' as a whole?"

"I intensely dislike this module, hey! I'm not really a technical person. What about you?"

When I was citing that phrase, a lad who was sitting next to Nosipho was packing his belongings, and he bounced the moment I completed the phrase with the question. Before Nosipho could answer, I gave her a 'wait a minute' signal with my palm subtending her face, as I went to fetch my backpack from the chair I staked out earlier.

I substituted the bloke, and gave Nosipho a pat on her shoulder to bespeak her into continuation. She then carried on by divulging her 'potential response', and said, "Okay! *Konje* what was the question? Oh! Yeah! If I dislike technical modules - well - I pretty don't hey. In actual fact, I love them! Even in high school I preferred EGD and CAT over Mathematics and Science. Technicality is the only way to life in our generation, hey! Think about it..."

"*Ai! Mbore hape...*"

"What's that?" Her face was dislocated, yet maintained its beauty. Confusion was written all over her facial expression...

"*Eisan*! Some phrases make complete sense when said in our home languages. Let me try... Well - *'Mbore hape'* is a Tswana Phrase meant to tell the other person in the dialogue to bore them again - showing how bored they are by their initial attempt. I hope it makes sense when I used technical English to explain it (laughing a little). *Andithi* y'all Nguni´s don't wanna learn Sotho Languages? Be embraced, 'cause with me, you gon' learn by force!" I tuned out my phrase with a smirk and few nods, dilating my eyelids to emphasize the level of seriousness in my notation, yet modifying little force.

"Are you kidding me?" She interjected, "I've always wannet to learn how to speak Tswana, Hao! I thought you colored or something. Wow! I have a study partner and he's Tswana? Look at God! Just take a proper look at Him!" We both laughed.

I then told her that we needed to commence with VBA Coding, since I never understood the lecturer and I hardly gave the module most of my regard.

She started from the lead off, explaining: Spreadsheet functions this, Array Formulas that, Algorithms this, Debugging that, VBA Coding this, Repetition/Loop structures that, Operators and Programming this, Subroutines versus Functions that, Binary digits this, IF-THEN-ENDIF- that, ...

In less than two hours, I had already gotten the concept. She sure knew how to explain...

"I only had breakfast today, what are we gonna eat?" She asked.

"I had my lunch before our session, so I'm just gonna have snacks or dessert."

"Oh! I might just have what you had for your lunch..."

"I didn't eat here - I was at Jo'burg Park."

"That's far. Why?"

"I had a meeting there, so we had it over lunch."

"*Manje* - what's gonna happen with your meal? Did you cancel?"

"Nah, hence I have to take snacks for now. Either way - my sponsor doesn't allow cancellation of meals, or - should I say: They don't refund for cancelled meals. So not utilizing would mean losing..."

"Shame - I have to consider myself blessed for being under CSIR, I guess - let's get going."

We had that small talk while packing our bags, then made our way to the dining hall. When we were walking towards the Matrix Door, an 'old friend' of mine hugged her. It was that colored guy who called me with Basie's phone.

"Nosipho! Long time, girl! *Waarhetjy* been hiding (where have you been hiding)?" He greeted her in delight.

"Oh! – Really? Sammy? You the one who had been low key lately! Being a father is keeping you jailed, huh?"

"Agh! *Nee* man, I've always been around," he said, turned his face towards me and continued to reluctantly address an extended greeting to me, "What's up *broer*?"

That greeting was chaperoned by an offering of *'Kho!'* (A fist for brotherhood greeting in South Africa) I responded chastely and openly, saying, "It's all well, bro, but we have unfinished business."

Nosipho, affected with wonder, intruded, "You guys know each other?"

I defensively reacted verbally, "I wouldn't say we - KNOW - each other, but we've met before. Bro - we really should have a talk. A talk that should solve this problem, not intensify it. Or *kanjani*?"

"*Broer,Ek* can't. *Ek* wanna, *maar ek* can't."

"*Mfwethu*, think about this - ..." Before I could finish my sentence, Nosipho complained, "Guys! I'm here - Hello? What's happening?"

"*Haek*! Maybe I should have a word with Basie! There's more to this than what meets the eye... Nosi, let's move hey -" I had to put an end to that time consuming 'get together'.

"*Nee! My broer - nee* man! Don't tell Basie, please! She'll press charges. This is big my *broer*, please! *Jy weet wat*(you know what) - let's just meet *laater* (later), *ses*O'clock, outside Chamber of mines. *Wat jy dink (what do you think)*?"

"Six O'clock? *Ayt*, cool... You better pitch and not be late! Nosi, let's..."

"*Awe broer, awe...*" He faded with his traditional conclusion. Coloreds were known for that phrase. It kind of made them sound and look cool when they cited it. Well - to an extent that even other tribes started using it to sound colored, or better yet to sound 'cool'. I had to admit that I also indulged in it before, and I reckoned it worked.

We then departed, walked through The Matrix and elevated to the Dining Hall. Nosipho was quiet and confused until we exited the elevator. After using our student cards to enter into the Dining Hall, she said, "MrSir, I know we only met yesterday, but - you can talk to me about anything. What's going on?"

"Nosi, Nosi, Nosi - nothing I can't handle is up, hey - now tell me, what are we gonna study after eating?"

Before she could reply - BZZ! BZZZ! BZZ! BZZZ!

"MrSir - Hello?"

"Hi MrSir, how are you?"

"I'm well, thanks - and how are you?"

"Couldn't be better... You're talking to Bella, and I'm recruiting for a school. I'm calling from a Recruitment Agency in Johannesburg, Marlboro, and I would love to have a face to face appointment with you for further details. When can you be available? Sir-"

"I - can't - say much now, uhm - how soon should it be? And - what is it about?"

"It's for winter classes and Saturday sessions. Mathematics, you are MrSir, right? A math facilitator... right?"

"On point... ma'am. Well - where will our appointment be?"

"Anywhere around Johannesburg... Sir! Where are you currently based?"

"In Braamfontein... Where are your offices?"

"Okay, let's do this, sir. I'll come to where you are to make things easy for you. Name a place, time and date. It has to be a public place, like a restaurant - over lunch or supper - all on me. What's your say?"

"Perfect! Jo'burg Park seems convenient for me. They also have a variety of restaurants and I'm not that picky - so you name the restaurant..."

"That's cool - I'll call you again to finalize our meeting and the restaurant. Thank you for your time, sir."

"You welcome. Enjoy the rest of your day, ma'am." Then I hung up.

"Yoh! You can be serious when you want, neh? What was that all about?" Out of eavesdropping, said Nosipho.

To cut it short, I just said, "Work -" to show little interest in sharing my business with her. She tried to suck it out of me, but she failed. After going back and forth with her inquisitive tendencies and my 'refusing to answer' goals, she dropped this on me, "So - tell me, how are you in alignment with knowing Sammy and the call you have just received? Who are you? What do you do for a living? Not that I was eavesdropping but..."

I quickly grabbed her defense by the collars and made her feel small by saying, "Well - you were actually eavesdropping, and it's rude. Dig up so we can go back to them books, *hao*!"

She changed the subject and indulged in talking about her family until we went back to the library. We then pushed, pushed and pushed with Computational Engineering until we both caught up with past papers as well.

It was around seven thirty post meridiem when we fetched our third meals of the day and went our separate ways. We were really done for the day, and I was content with how far we worked.

I remembered that I had to meet up with Sammy at six O'clock as I walked towards my flat, "*Eisan!*" I stood still, put my right hand on top of my head, and tried to figure out how I could arrange another meeting with him.

"Maybe Nosipho got his number, doesn't she?" I asked myself. Part of me said, "Ask her," and another said, "wait for tomorrow." I chose to wait for the following day, the latter won.

When I approached the door of my room, my auditory senses were smoothly swept by the sound of a playing keyboard. It was Toni. He would play it and sing the whole night when he rehearsed for his performances, but no music distracted me from sleeping, studying and writing.

I hollered at him, "Sup Dawg? What it do?"

"Na-ing major, just an intro' for tomow´s performance - any ideas?"

"Nah, I'm blank and - tired. I kinda had a long day, bruh. Where you performing? And what time?"

"A man gotta be tired to show that they living, bruh! It's gonna be at The Orbit, tomow eight thirty to be exact. Tag along, dawg."

"I don't think I'll make it, bro - I got exams coming up, and..."

"C'mon bro! We can spend just an hour then we bounce. It won't be time consuming, but worth it, I promise you, bro! You won't regret it. It's also gonna count for your poetry profile. Think about it."

I never believed in peer pressure. I never settled for anything that was against my wishes just to please a ´brother´. I was just not about that life, but - what he tried to convince me with was what I would have blinked upon even if he had not blown the air. I dug art and I would stop a heartbeat for it.

So I said, "*Ayt, ayt*! I hear you. So - what's the theme?"

"That's my *nikka*! Anything deep and dope will do - there's no specific theme. Coming to think of it - let's make a collab'. I sing, you recite your poem, -"

Word For The Record: 'Nikka' in South Africa is a cool word for Hip Hop fans, or rather for American life followers. They use it to call each other with no meaning attached to it. We, those who read and do research, know the history behind the word, but we still don't relate, and in our country the word is not offensive to any tribe and race. However, we use the word like nobody's business. I guess we really want to be part of America to an extent that we adopted and have adapted to their swag and anything they consider cool. 'Nikka' is derived from 'Negro', which was similar to 'Kafir' back in Apartheid era.

I replied, "*Jah neh*? Damn! We gonna kill this one!"

We gave each other fists of brotherhood as confirmation that we were really going to nail the performance that way. Then I insisted, "We gotta start writing now, dawg - my retention is too low to start any minute later."

"That's wah-I'm talkin' about!"

We wrote, rehearsed and edited, wrote, tweaked and rehearsed - until we eventually lost our energies to the pens. We nodded off...

Chapter O - Ownership of your life.

BZZZ! BZZZ! BZZZ!

"Eish! Uhm! Huuuiwii! Hello!"

"**G**ood morning MrSir, it's Bella. I'm sorry for waking you up. Can we have our appointment in two hours from now, over breakfast?"

"Oh! – Uhm! – Yeah, sure. - Which restaurant are we gonna have it in?"

"Wimpy will do. Exactly half past eight."

"Half past eight it is. 'til then..."

I received her call at around twenty three minutes past six ante meridiem. It was my cue to wake up, freshen up and gather my necessary documents for in case she required them.

Bella was a beautiful half-Indian-half-White lady who had her own Recruitment Co. Agency. She had that shiny long charcoal black hair which shone over her shoulders, mostly covering the sides of her soft, spotless tawny face which was composed of a long sharp nose, moderate sized pure white eyes with pitch black pupils, small pink lips, long chin and cheek bones which managed to complement her flat forehead.

She looked twenty five, which was eight years younger than her age. She was as short as I was, and as petit as Blessing was. If I had to disregard her age, I'd consider her my type. I'm talking about the most beautiful woman I had ever seen among her kind! Her voice was angelic and her smile could heal HIV. Owning a company was proof enough that she was smart and diligent. She chose to break out of the system at a young age.

It was when my wristwatch 'tick-tocked' towards eight ante meridiem, when I was already at Jo'burg Park. I was waiting for her.

I spent the whole thirty minutes sipping the Appletiser that I had ordered as an appetizer, and arranging all my documents.

Something behind my right eye told me to glimpse at the door, and I did. I saw a very attractive lady looking lost. She was asking the waiter if he had seen 'MrSir.' Since she said 'a man called MrSir' the waiter couldn't link me with the wanted man. I could hear their little conversation, so I just waved at her. She gave me a broad smile and literally raised her eyebrows.

She swerved across the tables and before she could reach ours, I stood up, pulled her chair out, waited for her to sit, gave her chair a gentle push towards the table and went back to mine.

"WOW! What - a - lovely - experience! Who's your mom? Thanks and good morning, MrSir!"

"...My mom? Why? Morning, Bella."

"She must be really proud of you! Not all mothers are blessed with such a smart, good looking gentleman as their son. Your appearance, also, doesn't match your profile - are you sure that you are MrSir?"

In my mind I laughed and said, "Who asks that?"

With composure, I externally just chuckled a little, and said, "Well - I guess I am. I don't blame you, though - I get that a lot, actually. You'll get used to me looking too young for my tasks. I have to admit that I didn't expect such beauty too - especially possessed by an 'owner' of a company. I'm impressed and inspired! A typical black person would ask: Whose gold did you dig? But you don't strike me as one of those who take shortcuts. Now tell me - when and how did you start?"

She smiled and asked if I wasn't in a hurry for anything before she summarized her story. I gave her the platform...

Bella used to be one of those party freaks during her teen years. She was playful and never took anything serious. Her extreme dislike for school was based on the idea that 'there was too much fun outside school than there was inside'. The only days she missed school or couldn't wait for the following school days were when she had intentions of flirting with boys in her class and upper classes.

Sometimes she took it to higher standards of flirting with her male teachers. Some days she would tell boys who were after her to bunk classes and promised them that whoever bunked more classes would win her, but the poor lads couldn't get the chance to 'really be' with her due to being expelled from school. So yes, there were poor blokes out there who couldn't finish schools as a repercussion of being lured by Bella's charm and beauty. Poor men!

"I mastered the art of using my appearance, tweaked it with a perfect smile, to get what I wanted. Both: in the streets – and - at home - MrSir. I used my innocent look to get away with a lot!" said Bella.

She passed Standard Ten (Matriculation) with an average mark of forty-nine per cent, and she felt like she could have done better, despite how frivolous she was. After collecting her matriculation statement, seeing that her results did not reflect her ability, she then wondered how she would make up for her past mediocre actions.

Word For The Record: Most people's performances aren't in proportion to their potential. Most people's abilities are greater than their results. We hardly do according to how we can, but according to how much effort we put in. Maybe it's time we started giving in the amount of effort equivalent to our potential!

She tried registering with a college to study Business Management, but she was rejected. Her smile, her beauty and her soft voice didn't do the magic on the application forms. All those external factors that worked in her favor did not mean a thing in the academic world. She was down for a route of staying home that year - and the slay queen in her started fading. Even blokes in her hood started becoming *sapiosexual*, and she was no longer a 'potential' in their eyes anymore. They were at different tertiary institutions and a 'home-staying' lady didn't look attractive anymore. Brains started counting more than looks.

All her friends were in Tertiary institutions - and subtly, the society started using her as an example of 'beauty with no brains'. The rate at which her value dropped was directly proportional to the rate at which she startled! She sure hit her rock bottom!

She started disregarding her looks and considered her eager to succeed. She knew very well that she had an option of relocating to a different town where no one knew her, to find herself a rich or just successful lad, but the God in her was bigger than her desire to take shortcuts. She asked herself one question, "What do you do when your considered ´only advantage´ no longer works for you?"

She remembered powerful words Rapulana Seiphemo once cited in the movie Jerusalem, "Adapt or die!"

She searched for a loophole in the world that required her purpose. However, finding one's purpose was easier said than done.

She said, "MrSir, the concept of self-introspection is often preached by every motivational speaker, but it is never stretched out to an extent that it could be deeply understood by the audience. People spend hours in mirrors, preening themselves, just to look 'stunning', but they never take a minute of reflecting their inner beauty, to feel stunning. See? All these ladies care more about how they look than who they really are...¨

She shook her head, showing deep relation to her story, and continued, ¨They get worried when their make-up washes away, but they never give a damn when their potential gets wasted. They show little to no care when they lose themselves in the process of impressing people. Often, they care more about how people feel about them than how they feel about themselves. They seek approval from people, instead of finding it from their own selves.How can I put it? It's like - if they aren't told that they are beautiful, then they won't tell themselves that they are..."

I remarked, "*Jah Neh*? Even if they told themselves that they are, they'd still not be convinced until someone else confirms. True, true..."

She went on, "You feel me! Unfortunately, MrSir, this is our society. This is the system we were born and raised in - and - I had to break out of it. I had to probe into who I really am. I detached the real me from my flesh and embarked on the journey of a thorough self-introspection. SELF-INTROSPECTION, MrSir, was my stepping stone. I started asking myself deep questions in shallow terms: Who am I? What do I love? What should I do with what I love? How do I change the world with what I love? How would the world respond to the change brought by what I love? Can I make a living out of what I love? What are my limitations? What would deter and detain me from being the best in the field? What is my special talent, knowledge, skill or ability that is aligned with what I love? Is there a loophole in the world that needs me? Is the loophole aligned with what I love? Am I willing to do what I love 'til I turn grizzled? Does the One above approve what I love? Can what I love be my purpose? You get where this is going, right? Such questions spun in my head, MrSir."

As she was citing, I was connecting the dots, trying to answer those questions internally. They were deep, but I was following her lead. However, she did not wait for my intrapersonal conversation. She was flowing, getting deep into the concept – she said, "I started viewing things with a different eye. I became a self-motivated critical thinker. I said my 'byes' to involving myself in unimportant conversations and gave negative, shallow thinkers a wide berth to. I would rather watch Educational Television Programmes than follow these time-consuming soapies..."

Her story brought life to a poem I collaborated with *Poetic B* later in our lives. The title of the poem was: *How To Come Back,* and it went like this...

(Poetic B)
Okay! Okay! I can explain.

(MrSir Placidfray)
Explain what? You are too dressed up for someone who's going to bed. Are you sneaking out?

(Poetic B)
But....

(MrSir Placidfray)
Okay! No buts! Go back to your room and this is not a debate.

(Poetic B)
[interjections]

(Poetic B)
I feel like a bird trapped in a cage.
I'm fuming with rage.
This is just a passing phase, right?
Then I guess I have reached the stage.

This is the 21st century.
A different version of Adam and Eve.
Funny how the society always gets to have a say in how I live my life
Yet they know nothing about me.

I still don't understand why you treating me like an enemy.
Explain why you are angry at me for being in love.
If you really cared about me you would understand how I really feel,
Instead you are angry at me for loving someone.
It's crazy how we were both conceived in one woman's body.
I guess sharing a womb was all in vain...

(MrSir Placidfray and Poetic B)
...Look how we fail to reach an understanding!

(Poetic B)
Brother, your love tends to hurt.
See if I was free
I wouldn't have sneaked out.
But because your way of life
Is based on ancient times
My heart was captured by an outsider's love.
If I was well treated,
I wouldn't have had to find someone else to validate my worth.

It is not my intention to sound disrespectful
Try to turn the page
A lot has changed
Females are no longer slaves
Because we seem to differ

So I can say we are not the same.

Our place is no longer in the kitchens
Child bearing is not our only mission
See we have our own virgin decisions
We have realized the importance of owning our grounds.
So you think your girl didn't sneak out?

Our parents let you out but hers didn't.
Is it justified when it is done for you?
Well your kinda loving isn't fair.
We all sneaked out
That's because we feel locked up.
This isn't love, it fails to protect
Though it managed to keep us locked up in a cage.
I'm sorry I sneaked out.
I found it as a way to find love...

(MrSir Placidfray and Poetic B)
HashTag Men Are Trash...

(MrSir Placidfray)
... is based on a huge sample space.
The generalization might be hasty,
But more than half of us aim for dustbins!

I know me better - and I know my gender,
You have no idea what you are getting yourself into!
Talking about "doing it for love" - you are in no age for intimacy,
Your psychological make up is not ready to handle hurt,
I'm protecting you from aches
I know your system can't fight against.

And don't even dare pin it on my girlfriend - see? She's
Blessed to have a man, but you on the other hand, you
Are risking your emotional health for a boy -
Who doesn't even guarantee you a future.
Let's do this - tell him you are pregnant,
And see how many "Athletes"
Masked with "I'm your man" we have in this world.

(MrSir Placidfray and Poetic B)
Our judgements are eclipsed by our sexual differences,
Our intentions for each other's concern are misinterpreted due
To a variation of chromosome selection during meiosis,
We have one thing in common -
we are both very much opinionated...

(MrSir Placidfray)
But you are my mother's daughter,
A strand of RNA without me -
My advice should form protein to your well-being -
Open your mind so I can feed you with wisdom,
I've been around - Let us be our DNA!

I'm only responsible for what I say,
Not how you take it...

You just can't expect me to allow you to fall for
A guy who won't stick around after making a howler.
The mistakes that may affect us as your clan,
and most importantly, which will affect
your future relationships and success.
Did love blind you so much that logic has become bombast?

This is what makes it easy for our folks
To give me an emancipation to do
what they hinder you from doing.

In this Anno Domini era - trust is scarce -
But women are too weak to be stingy with it –
I'm gonna have to help you save some
For your future husband.

Don't allow yourself to learn from experience
What you can learn in theory and experiment.
Look around...

My concern is not focused on what you do,
But where and who you do it with.
I know how we blokes are -
I'm afraid you'll end up in the hands of a guy

Whose tendencies are of a child.

No one promised anyone fairness -
Don't heed that -
Ask yourself if what isn't considered fair is worth it.

It's basically a matter of Control over Emotions,
What do you think muscles are for?
Men aren't meant to be soft,
We use our minds to digest thoughts
But y'all give your hearts the same job.

An intention of a man
Is the limiting reactant to all rapports -
And how women respond is a catalyst -
The reaction can still take place without your intention,

Basically...

We are in the X-axis - independent,
I'm sorry if I sound like I support patriarchy.

We know what we want,
and when we have it,
we are responsible for
Having it stick around.

But you ladies, my lil sister, you...
Your ability to last in any relationship is limited
By what his intentions are with you.

And still...

Nothing is guaranteed!

That on its own makes up more than 50% of my insecurities -

Insecurities of seeing my lil sister's happiness
Cradled in an outsider's hands - an outsider who
Doesn't even come forward and show signs of solemnity
And commitment.

I'm sorry, but you not going anywhere - not 'til I know him - not
Until I can trust that he is here to stay, or at least -
Not until I feel like you'll be the wrong one in your break up...
I know that...

(MrSir Placidfray and Poetic B)
Mistakes are lessons for future endeavors...

(Poetic B)
...How lonely is a journey alone?
I'm expected to take part in no relation
Yet at some point I'm...

(MrSir Placidfray and Poetic B)
...Supposed to build a home...

(MrSir Placidfray)
...With a bloke who won't take your innocence?
Did you forget that the bride price is supposed
To be paid by your "first time"?
My sister, treasure yourself!
Instead of sneaking out,
Go and read Exodus chapter 22, from verse 16
I'm astonished by your obstinacy...
I'm not gonna let my gut down, but....

(MrSir Placidfray and Poetic B)
As much as you cannot stop
a child from going to hell,
The least you can do is teach
Them How To Come Back to heaven!

She continued, "I started reading novels, newspaper articles, magazines and online articles. I *'googled'*, *'googled'* and *'googled'*, searching for answers to a question derived from the self-introspection.The question was: Who contributes most to a learner's performance between a learner and a teacher? I wanted to know what the major contributor needs in order to maximize their contribution and ensure a good pass. If it's a teacher, then why aren't learners passing? Did the problem lie with bad teachers or with the school's management for hiring bad teachers? How do you know if a teacher is good or bad? What makes a good teacher? I *'googled'* such questions, MrSir. I started prioritizing consuming knowledge over having fun. In fact, consuming knowledge and deciphering a cryptic situation became fun for me. It became more fun than getting drunk and turning up the whole night, 'cause at least I would not wake up messy and in headaches from hangovers. I'm not against anything alcoholic - don't get me wrong - I'm against alcohol abuse. I'm against drinking to fill a stomach with no purpose of celebration or something. Drinking your last few bucks is stupid, to me. I still indulge in wines here and there, but on special occasions, MrSir, because successful people know when to drink, how much to drink and where to drink. Unlike people who have not figured out that there's meaning to every action. But let me not dwell too much into this drinking topic."

That kind of made me wonder if drinking was necessary for celebrations, but I let it slid as she continued, "MrSir – if I didn't know who I am, I'd just be a useless beautiful woman without a purpose, who depends on a particular man for a living. I'd be living a lie, thinking that drinking and dancing the whole night every weekend is the ultimate pleasure a 'normal' person should utilize. I'd be relying on getting laid, fed and drunk in order to be 'happy'. I'd be thinking that life is all about getting married, having a family, taking orders from my husband so as to not get 'kicked out of his house', raising his kids when he's busy serving his purpose - Blah! Blah! Blah! I - ain't - about - that - life, MrSir! That's a systematic life! It's ingrained in the society to believe that when God said that women are helpers, He meant or implied that they should be housewives. I'm a different believer, MrSir, according to me, helping means contributing. Contribution comes in different ways. One of them is through creating employment for those men whom we are supposed to 'help'. I chose to be my own boss - and I have both men and women working for me. My business is simple and interesting, and I love it. My business is my purpose."

I was nodding a lot, while digging in as she went on, "The loophole in the system was that schools' management teams always hire teachers based on their academic achievements, not on how they relate and connect with the learners - not on how they can break down a complex matter for learners. Teachers are good teachers based on their ability to make learners understand complex contents of a subject, not on what they know and have achieved at school.So - MrSir - my agency is just a bridge between schools and good teachers. Not just teachers, but good teachers - Not only good teachers, but facilitators too. There's a difference between teachers and facilitators - and we go for facilitators, and we also make facilitators out of teachers where necessary."

I then asked myself if they weren´t the same. It was few years later when I understood the difference. (Facilitators simplify, teachers introduce.) She continued, "In my agency - we recruit, critically analyze, argue why the facilitator deserves a post, no favors - then Tada! The school hires only the best through us. All schools signed with us produce *hunnid* percent pass rates with quality results every year. We are breaking out of the system, MrSir. I probed your profile and I see you as one of the best facilitators around. Are you willing to break out of the system with us? Here's your contract - along with claim forms through us. Question is: - ..."

She took a glimpse at her wristwatch, sipped her cappuccino and sealed her speech, "Will you join the crew of best facilitators and facilitate at the school I'm recruiting for?"

I was taken - I was motivated - I was lured - I was inspired - I was... I was willing to join the crew, but - temporarily. Not to be a party pooper, but I fell in love with the concept of 'being my own boss' more. I started wondering what my purpose was. I asked myself the same questions she asked herself before she started the Agency.

In response to her proposal, I told her that I was in, but I had to first read the contract and consult with legal advisors. We agreed that I'd e-mail the signed documents the following evening.

We ate during her story citation, so by the time she proposed the post; we were already through with our breakfast. She settled the bills when I was packing up the documents, ready to disperse. When I arrived at my room, I wrote a motivational article, applying my agricultural knowledge, inspired by the breakfast, before I received a ´please call me´ message.The title of the article was: *Like A Tree*, and it went like this...

Chapter P - Planting motivation with tree's qualities (article)

A simple living creature like a tree is strong enough to resist all the seasons that aren't in its favor to produce fruits, patient and persistent enough to wait for that season that is its to produce. Do Orange trees die in summer? Do peach trees die in winter? NO! They are persistent with what they want, which is the production of their fruits.

You also might be in your winter times if you are a peach tree, but if you stand as firm as it does, you'll surely reach summer and grow back the leaves you lost in august. You didn't lose them because you not God's favorite, but because they would've been a disturbance in your process of growing new fresh ones to optimize your production.

You lost friends you had when you were in primary school, did that affect your school performance? You'll still lose people who used to be close to you in high school, at tertiary too, never to forget at work. But, know that it's a way of optimizing your performance. You are going through hard times in life, I don't know much about those hard times, but I assure you that those times are the ONLY way to reach your destination, only if you won't give up.

If you cut a tree's roots, you'll destroy it. If it's lucky enough not to die, it shall instead be weak. You cannot cut its root to make it strong, you either cut them to kill it or to make it weak. Instead, the roots grow deeper into the soil to help the tree to be stronger and to help it absorb even more minerals for its production and its growth.

But there are things that you can remove from a tree to make it look better, to make it to give you what you want and to make it survive harsh environmental conditions. You can shake it off to remove its leaves, you can cut some of its branches to shape it according to the way you want its shade to be like, or you can cut the unproductive branches so that it does not lose its minerals on the branches that do not produce, sparing those minerals for productive branches.

That is a tree. Compare your life with it and question yourself why it can live longer than us? There are things that you should not change in your life, or cannot change in your life. You cannot change your historical make-up. You cannot change your family. Now what is it that you shouldn't change? The answer is within, your belief system. Your religious belief is your root. If you change what you believe in, you are cutting your roots, you'll either be spiritually destroyed or weak.

Stick to what you believe in and grow your relationship with It/Him. It can be God, your ancestors, your own created "supreme being" whatever, but for so long as you have faith, it's or He will work for you. I believe in God, and He's working for me. I'd urge you to believe in Him too but it's your choice.

The things you can change are how you study, how you view your life, your friends, your responses to the environment and to people, your actions, your thoughts, you name them. It's permissible to change them if they are working for you, but it is an obligation to change them if they aren't. It's mostly in our last minutes when we realize how significant and counting a second is. Edit your life the way you'd edit your tree to bare fruits.

What you leave behind you is a symbol of the existence of your soul. You can have a garden full of different trees, but they'll not produce equally or the same thing unless they are 100% identical. The farmer or the gardener will always cherish and value each one of them, accordingly.

There are billions of us in this world. Each and every one of us has their own purpose in life. Our Gardener (In my perspective, it is God) knows what production we were planted for. We can never occupy the same position and space. Thus: Value what you can do and what you love without heeding what someone else does and says. We were born to be different. No matter how much we try to be the same, the more we will be even more different to each other and to who we originally ought to be.

Different trees have different structures. Each form of the structures tells us about the type of the tree, its habitat, its function and its production. Without going deep into Agriculture, we all know that you can tell if a tree is in good form to bare a certain quantity of production by just looking at its shape (structure). If the tree doesn't have leaves (mostly green), it is less likely to produce since the leaves contain chlorophyll which takes a crucial part in the production process. You can never expect Watermelon to be produced by a tree that grows vertically upwards for we know that the size and mass of a watermelon is huge. So the structure of a watermelon tree was made to creep on the ground to suit what it produces.

This is what is happening with us. We have different characters, different points of views, different physiques, different IQ Levels, different habits, the list is long. With all those differences, we should categorize ourselves with which purposes we should serve when we are planted with these structures on earth.

Like a tree, are we going to serve our purposes according to the way we were genetically and spiritually made or we are going to try fitting in other people's purposes by tending to make their dreams ours or by living their lives? Take heed that you do not make howlers over what you can fix now. Be as unique, productive and purpose serving as a tree. If you know yourself, if you know what type of a tree you are, relocate to your habitat where you will maximize your production and live Like A Tree. Just like that...

Chapter Q - Q, A, R type of debate (Leticia)

Lost in the agricultural fantasy of my article, my heed was grinded to a turn of events by a 'please call me' message from Leticia. I called her back, and...

"Hey... You..." She answered.

"...A callback? ...Really? Leticia?" I teased.

"...Student life! Hey!" Then we laughed in relation.

"How have you been doing though? ...Long time -" I said.

"How have I - Mhm! - Exactly the reason why I sent a callback. *Hape wena* you never run out of airtime, or things changed? Tell me - do you know Sammy? Sammy Toe 'n Beng?"

Boom! Leticia was the last person I expected to be associated with Sammy - or as a matter of fact - the last person to reach out to me after such a long time we had last spoken. Could she be asking about the colored guy? I could only wonder...

Without further ado - an introduction of Leticia into my life took place before I met Condolences. Leticia was my ex. She was my high school *'regte'* (An Afrikaans derived slang word for someone you are committed to - in a relationship), but we were in a long distance relationship which seemed impossible to succeed without being tempted *comme ci comme ca* (here and there - derived from French). That was an excuse of course, we had all, at some point, been young and stupid, hadn't we?

We met when I was about to finish my tenth grade, during a provincial level of a debating competition at Lydenburg, Mpumalanga. My debating team consisted of three confident girls and five reasonable boys. Two boys and one girl were in their tenth grade, and the rest were in their twelfth. Eleventh graders did not make it to the main team - I guess we (the tenth graders - first generation of the born frees) were that good.

The motion of the debate was: Age concerning statutory rape should be fixed at sixteen.

It was a juicy theme for high school learners! Leticia and I were second speakers from different schools. The setting of the debate was set up in such a way that after introductions, 'you - ask - I - answer - and - I - ask - you - answer' was a system of exchanging propositions and oppositions. The opposition team was the one that started first and my school was in the proposition side.

We had beaten all other schools we were against - so did Leticia's school. So it was a final stage for that level. One of the rules, which made it even more interesting, was that the chances of second speakers for speaking were not limited by time, but by 'running out of facts, questions and logic' and by 'surrendering'. Adjudicators had a way of putting a cease to a 'getting pointless' Q and A session.

The organizers were smart enough to align boys against girls from one speaker to another, and I was against a very beautiful, obstinate and smart girl - Leticia!

She started with her salutations and went on with her opposition, "I believe that eighteen as it is - is still below the average age for maturity. A sixteen year old girl is a fragile and pliable teenager whose heart and mind may easily be coaxed into doing anything by any older sycophant. She can be towed by any old rope that looks tight and stable in her eyes - but - the outcomes are never in her favor. Her losses are always irreplaceable. Her body may recover, but her mind and heart may not, including her reputation...

Ladies and gentlemen, the experience forms part of her growth - she is still growing for crying out loud! Isn't that type of 'pleasure' for grown-ups? We are living in the twenty first century, where men see these girls as 'easy objects for quenching thirst'. How do we expect a girl who is still struggling to understand the basic concepts of a grade ten subject to understand the meaning and perks of 'pleasure'?

The emotional, hormonal - all in all psychological - religious and physical involvements experienced in the activity are complex and sticky for adults. How do - we - then - expect a sixteen year old to break them down? She may look old enough to know what she wants, but she's definitely not old enough to know what she needs. She's not yet fully developed to a level of having the ability to comprehend the pros and cons of her choices. She's not sponsored by Sanlam - she - can - not - think ahead! She's merely amenable to anything that thrills her without considering the long term impacts.

Eighteen years is a convenient age, not a perfect one. Going below it is not a solution in any logical form, but a problem. Ladies and gentlemen - the age concerning statutory rape must either be fixed on eighteen or above. Not sixteen! Thank you..."

I was touched, I felt like changing sides. I was in fact taken - I - felt - her! She actually devalued my preparations - she was a few levels above my expectations. Did she bury me alive?

T-CUP (Thinking Carefully Under Pressure) was my last resort. I could only pray that it would work. I tried ad libbing, splashing her picture of painting girls as victims in relationships dull...

After my salutations, I proposed, "An interesting question rises from the opposition team: Is statutory rape a punishment for girls' bad choices, but implemented on men? If a young naughty and silly girl, with a physical appearance of an older woman - forward enough to make a move on a lad - seduces an older lad, should the guy always ask for her ID before he can act upon his hormonal reactions? Oh - and - BTW - girls under 18 never divulge their true age! Especially if he meets her in a club - the same 'clubs' with 'no persons under the age of 18 are allowed' signs on entrances…

Leaderships - these girls are street smart, naughty and they grow faster than men. They sure know what they want - and - age has nothing to do with 'knowing what you need'. Adults also don't know what they need. Even our honorable parents file for divorce every single day, showing us that they know what they want, but 'definitely not what they need'.

A teenager is her own person, and it is her character that should determine her deeds and choices. Men can't be scapegoats of these young girls' choices. If the body is ready - so is the mind - and - heart. An unready person knows when they are not ready, and they should say. Without going broader - girls are different. Under normal circumstances, a sixteen year old who gets involved with an older man, without being forced, but by being consensually convinced into being involved, is not a victim of any sort of rape. She is actually guilty of not abstaining and temptation!

Ladies and gentlemen, I believe that sixteen is a better age - but not perfect. I wish it went a little lower to thirteen, I mean - after twelve is ..."

Then the audience completed my phrase with, "lunch!" Then the whole auditorium laughed and applauded when I bowed in gratitude and conclusion of my proposition. I was simple and shallow, but I made my point. My 'word choices' were not 'posh' but my points were clear to both illiterate audience and nerds. My aim subtly shifted from impressing them with my vocabulary to being understood. As much as I was supposed to stoop to everyone's level, despite the fact that I ad libbed, because for some reason I felt like introductions were directed to adjudicators and the audience, I would still admit that Leticia's introduction was better than mine, but...

My opponent was intimidated by my ability to lure the audience, and that kind of shook her retaliation. Her confidence was disturbed. Even so, I could sense that she underestimated my intellectuality and I was ready to bounce back with elements of surprise.

When the Master of Ceremony (MC) said, "QAR (Question - Answer - Retaliate) Session may commence! M'villa MST Academy, you have the honor to break the ice as the proposer."

I stood up with confidence, pierced her eyes with mine, moved to the centre of the stage, smirked and started, "I heard your antithesis clearly, ma'am, but not clear enough to: agree and not have questions. Between a sixteen years old virgin whose innocence may be hurled into the palms of an older bloke and the one whose innocence may be snapped by her peer, which one is innocent, a victim and didn't have a choice to say 'No'? And - why?"

She took about five seconds saying, "Well, uhmmm..." trying to comprehend my question. She then answered with, "The one who gets involved with an older man. That's what statutory rape is, isn't it? Would you not lay charges when a thirty year old man happens to help himself with your sixteen year old daughter?"

The level of control and confidence I possessed made me smile before I replied. I slowly said, "I'm not content with your answer - but well..." Then I stole a sight of adjudicators, pressing the bottom of my neck with my shoulders in an 'I don't know' sign, when they shrunk their faces, noting my points, and I continued, "To answer your question - I wouldn't press changes. I would instead blame myself for not raising my child well. In fact - I would reprimand her for making wrong and bad decisions, especially if she was willingly involved. Shouldn't we spread the advice of 'taking responsibility for your own actions' to our children instead of protesting for 'violation of unreasonable slash flawed rights'? The man would be innocent. What we don't love should not always be illegal. Now answer this open-mindedly: What do you say about girls who reject their peers, claiming that they have no cars, cash and the sundry to meet their demands? Are they also victims if they find older blokes who 'meet their demands'?"

She felt the heat and her voice started having scratches. In her emotional response, she said, "Those girls are young! Those older blokes should be responsible enough to reject them..."

I interrupted her with, "Reject them? Oh! So they aren't 'too young' to deal with rejection?"

The audience giggled in a low pitch when she defensively responded, "Pleasure and rejection are two different things. Can I ask my question without being interrupted?"

"I'm sorry but - if your arguments are focally based on age, then almost everything that has a psychological impact on a teenager should be a crime - leadership, your arguments are absurd. It's not age that is a problem here - but responsibility. Can't we teach that at schools? 'Cause, ladies and gentlemen, according to leadership here - rejection is also a crime. Now poor blokes are always caught up between hard places and rocks. It's not really about age - it's about character. People are different. Men shouldn't suffer the repercussions of reacting to nature preceding someone else's bad decisions. Anything that isn't against anyone's Will, should not be crime! Change your premises, ma'am!"

She was quiet and her eyes glinted with tears. I was beginning to feel sorry for her. So I continued with a lenient attack, "What about young adults who are about - say - twenty years old - who want to be committed? Can't he go for a 16 years old girl? I doubt you would mind such an age difference yourself, yet you oppose the motion. Ma'am, age concerning statutory rape should be fixed at sixteen. Surrender your side!"

She threw in the towel and said, "I surrender. I accept the motion," then she hid her face behind her palms, wiping her tears and went back to her seat.

The whole theatre hall was in uproar, applauding and screaming. My team ran to the stage and 'squealed in delight'. It was just magic. I glanced at Leticia and she was applauding too - as if she accepted defeat wholeheartedly. I was glad she did not take it personal - or at least that was what I thought...

Surrendering was her best option because losing with 'surrendering' had a better prize than losing with pure judgement. The organizers probably believed that one who surrendered showed qualities of reasonableness and the ability to know when to stop.

After the whole chaos of celebration cooled down, before the time of announcements of results (slash) handing over prizes, I went up to her. I gave her a hug without saying much and pleaded to see her after the closure of the event.

I said, "I need to teach you howta not gimme a tough time - 'cause you sure were close outchea hey! I need to meet your researcher as well - your introduction was top notch!" We laughed and she accepted my pleading. Networking was always my aim in school events, competitions and trips, but that one was an exception. My aim for asking for numbers was rather more personal and private than for networking. I was lured, captivated and, and, and...

It was the only debate that felt personal to me in my entire life - for I was against my crush (who eventually became my girlfriend) and I didn't let her win. I guess I never mixed business with pleasure! That - was - how - I - met - Leticia...

The contents of the Debate gave birth to a poem which I featured *Poetic B* on, later in life. The title of the poem was: *Check That Pole,* and it went like this...

(MrSir Placidfray)
All rise!
All sit!

(Instrumentals...)

(Poetic B)
I'm sickened
I feel like vomiting
I'm disgusted
It's annoying
So full of harassment
I wonder how you sleep at night
Knowing very well that you murder dreams

How dare you disrespect parents like that?
Do you think they would appreciate knowing how you
Get in between thighs of their precious offsprings?

They consider you a second parent
Yet you have the nerve to make them
Your manhood satisfaction objects,
What a pervert!

Agg sies man!
I hope you choke on the success
From your business of selling dreams!

I am certain that you promised them stability,
Love - affection - more or less - a bright future.
Poor innocent souls fell for words so sweet yet bitter.

I don't get how you can plant your haploid
Into an ampulla of the very same girl you

Teach and rebuke to heed teenage pregnancies!

Can they be that blind -
Or is it that you have the fold?

You make my hackles rise!
Your life deserves to be put on hold.

This is a violation of the same children's rights,
Your generation fought for two decades ago!

Aren't you ashamed of being a villain in a story line
That you should be crossing as a hero?

I don't even care about the "why you doing it"
And the "what could have led to it!"
You were supposed to be a home for them,
Not a pimp to your own satisfactions!

Nothing can substitute your disgrace -
No excuse, reason or justification can sound
Positive to be worth my attention at this point,
Your deeds are in the third Quadrant -
"All Students TAKE Control"
Now I see why you always TAKE
From those your job describe to give!

I'm not only hurt and disturbed by your
Level of selfishness and immaturity,
But by your lack of professionalism and humanity.

Put yourself in those thorny boots you tailored!
How would you feel if it was your daughter?

Jury - honourable judges of the Law - I don't think
He deserves freedom - 'cause clearly,
He showed unlimited ability to use it against people!

Anyone who uses democracy to suppress
People's rights doesn't deserve to live in
A free Society -

If not exile, then jail -
I rest my case!

(MrSir Placidfray)
Jury of the Court -
Judges of the Law,
And lovers who understand bonds,

I present to you - a perception!
Before you raise objections,
Ad Hominem should not be committed,
Fallacy of Ambiguity should be given a wide berth.

Answers to my questions will divulge all,
Before you heed the grain of grass on his eyelid,
Check that Pole in your eyeballs!

How old is your dad?
(73)
How old is yourself?
(36)
I reckon you not the first born at home...
Now - how old is your mother?
(50)

We are living in the 21st century!
Can you say women ovulate at an early age
As opposed to back in the days?

Take your time, as I continue in its mean...

Check the age differences,
How do you expect him to not walk
In his father's steps?
He's definitely just searching for "The One" -

Oh - "he's taking their future"
Doesn't your mom have a future now?

'Cause hey - we all know that our parents
Have the same age difference, if not a larger one!

Check that pole!

And your moms had y'all at younger ages too -

Check that pole!

All I'm saying is - y'all judge these old
Folks for dating young ladies - as
If they are forcing them - forgetting that
This type of relationships are responsible
For your birth,

And now your parents are -
"Happily ever after!"

Happily married - caamaaan!

I'm sorry if I sound like an activist,

Or...

A womanizer,

Or a feminist,

Or...

Whatever!

I'm just saying - Check that pole!

Don't get me wrong - I'm not saying seeing
A teacher and a learner in a car doing all
The "lovie dovie" stuff
Gives pleasure to my eyes -
it's not a nice picture...

Trust me -

It's disgusting,

But - so is the picture of seeing
any adult couple kissing in public,

There's nothing "ncaaaw" about it -

We should all respect ourselves -
I mean: What are bedrooms for?

All I'm saying is -

What they do behind closed doors,
Is none of our Tuck shops!

These young ladies know their rights,

I mean -

How do you explain the fact that
Teachers no longer hit them,
When they don't turn in their homework?

Oh - ya'll gonna claim they do nonsense in your absence?

Don't act like you not scared of your child yourself!

We both know you don't hit them when they are disobedient!

Check that pole!

These male teachers who go out with these
Kids aren't really doing anything wrong,
Unless it's done out of force.

So - in my conclusion I propose -

This man here is being a hunter -
He's going after what his heart desires,
He's looking out for his manhood,

He's aiming at enlarging his own hood,

Study your history, see how human species operate,
how our ancestors built homes.
Pay your origins a visit, and before you take him to jail,
Please - check that pole!

(Poetic B and MrSir Placidfray)
No one is right - no one is wrong!
Before we judge each other -
Before we think of removing sticks
In our fellow's eye - we should start
With the man in the mirror!
Reflect and Check That Pole!

Chapter R - Reaching the connection.

Leticia was one of the best students in her LLB class, when she called. I could reckon that the debates she participated in when we were in high school were more of passion to her than they were to me. She was all about arguments,research and the sundry - for a living!

Well - her loss in our last debate was desiccated for whatever illogical reason up until she saw one of her bosses in her 'practical company' paging through a case file with my name as an opponent. She saw it as an opportunity to retaliate, and - well - the bitter ex in her was also kind of resuscitated. Her boss allowed her to take the case and it led to our conversation...

"... Do you know Sammy? Sammy Toe 'n Beng?" She asked.

"Sammy? - The colored guy? The one Basie cheated me with?"

Her response accelerated my blood flow, "Yeah - the colored one - wait! Your ex cheated with him? Something doesn't add up here. Did you know that he wanted to kill you, and for some unreasonable circumstance he happened to have 'shot the wrong guy' - according to the police report. What's happening?"

I was thrown into a state of disarray - garbled and dashed. In my reception, I postulated, "Wait! What? You are not for real, are you?"

"I'm frank, real, and truthful - you can add to the list - MrSir. I'm also tryna add one and two about his case - your name appeared on the files and..."

"Leticia - I ain't got time for games, *ayt*?"

"I'm serious like a donkey right now!" Then we muzzled with reluctant laughter. I was actually amazed by the atmosphere she set with a reminder of one of my old lousy jokes. I'd say she missed me if I was that egotistic - maybe I was, maybe I wasn't - you'd just never know...

After trimming the gaggle - I said, "I - can't really say I know him. He's just a bloke in my past that happened to have hit where I was chowing. In fact, Basie cheated me with him and I caught them red handed in my room. Since then..."

"Wait a sec'! Did you just say in your room?"

"Yeah - long story hey... Since then, cryptic and peculiar *ish* had been popping in my life. It's like I'm haunted by a demon or something - I don't know. I can't make sense of anything right now. It's draining, Leticia - it sucks the energy outta my system *errday*! I just never thought *ish* was that deep for a bloke to even wanna kill. *Hai - noh - mahn*! There's more to this than what meets the eye."

"But, MrSir - why would he wanna kill ya? I mean - you caught them cheating on you, not the other way round, right? You weren't the side guy - so... Nah - something doesn't add up. Unless.... Wait - whatchu got on him?"

"Why do I feel like I'm being interrogated now? Ain't I suppose'da be the victim here? Where is he as we speak? Wait - damn! Are you representing him?"

"*Yana* - I'm obliged to, MrSir. I need your coordination."

"Wow! You - gotta - be - kidding me!" Then I hung up.

My head's temperature rose - so I had to alleviate the pending headache before it could result in a migraine by putting away the book I wrote the article on, and meditated. While humming my favorite song (*Bonang ho hlahileng marung*) in the nucleus of the meditation, I was struck by a sting of luminosity.

I remembered chronological occurrences which led me to constructing conditional arguments. I thought to myself while meditating, "If I hadn't met Nosipho and studied with her, I wouldn't have met Sammy again and I wouldn't have known his name. To top it off - I wouldn't have made an appointment with him. Mhm! In actual fact, if Nosipho and I didn't study 'til I missed the appointment, I'd have been a dead man."

I was stuck between two contradictory premises. My mind tried to break them down, "One - if Nosipho knew Sammy, then somehow they probably work together... Two - if they do work together, surely Nosipho would have made sure that I didn't miss the appointment with Sammy." It didn't add up...

All incidents sounded like Hocus-Pocus to me. I refused to be susceptible to the plight. My purpose started permeating every neuron of my brain. I knew that the Supreme Being's ways of clamping down on impediments weren't up for discussion. To all my loose socks, He appeared as my garter.

I went out of my understanding, ceased the meditation, reached out to my Bible and gasped for an antidote. Part of me said, "Just go to campus and study... Your brain will break this down in the absence of your attention to it. Get distracted..."

I followed my guts and packed everything. In a trice, I was already in campus, in the lab and trying to commence with my studies. I thought to myself, "Plead for focus, so you can grasp..." Then I closed my eyes for few seconds. As I was praying for focus, absent from reality, there appeared a pale hand waving in my face…

"Amen!" said Nosipho.

I sighed, smiled and said, "Hi Nosipho - I actually have questions for you..."

"I also wanna ask something - I read *Vuselela* this morning and it stated that Sammy is at a police station, charged with murder. Do you know anything about this case? I hope it's not the reason why I found you praying... MrSir - I'm..."

"*Vuselela*? Ehh! But - well - would I be wrong to believe that you could be his associate? I don't know what to think anymore - and - with *errthang* that had been happening in my life recently, I can't afford to be gullible."

"…His associate? - Gullible? MrSir - whatchu on about?"

"It's kinda logical to assume that I was supposed to be the target - he probably shot the wrong guy. But - we both know that validity isn't always aligned with reality. I can't base my conclusions on mere speculation."

I had to go all 'philosophical' on her. My intention was to repatriate her back to her place as just my 'study partner', not my lawyer. I did not trust her with the truth and my future blueprints.

Because philosophy wasn't her strong point, she kept her response short, "Oh! I see! So what are you going to do, MrSir?"

"Unless the law involves me on this case, I won't do anything. We got exams coming up, don't we?"

"Such focus is to die for. Since I'm still alive, it's a sign that I still have a looong way! You starting to motivate me, MrSir, let's start..."

"Wait -..." I checked if it was vibration that I thought I felt in my pockets. Unfortunately, there was no sign of any missed calls and messages, when I passed a sight onto my phone's screen. It was then when I realized that my subconscious side was expecting Leticia to call me again. Somehow her retaliation unzipped a gash that she left after our break up. However - it was water under the bridge...

We studied Critical Thinking: Sci-fi movies this, history behind the geographical structure of Johannesburg that, Poems this... When we were done with the concept, we treated Tutorial questions like *Witsies*, we treated Past papers, and so on...

It was around 4p.m when our brains notified us that we had enough for the afternoon. "Tomorrow afternoon? Continue?" I asked. She nodded while yawning and I asked further, "Do you play chess?"

"Who doesn't? You wanna get lashed?" She made a subtle, but frivolous, threat while leaning her cheeks on her fist, with her elbow on the computer desk, facing me as if she wanted to make a 'detective intentions' eye-contact.

"Oh! Well..." Before I could finish the sentence, I felt a vibration in my pockets. When I reluctantly checked, thinking it could be an 'imagination hoax' again - Bang!

"MrSir, speaking - how may I help you?"

"My *broer - ek* is in your flat now, KSI, waiting for *jy*. *Ek* want us to *praat* (talk), my *broer - Eksal* (I will) explain *ehhthing*. *Wat tyd* will *jy be hier* (here)?" It was Sammy!

I immediately hung up - scared for days! According to my assumptions, he was supposed to be at the police station, charged with murder - but then there he was - waiting for me at my flat! Could that be happening? I could only wonder, worry...

It felt like a dream and after pinching my left arm as usual, reality knocked on my forehead and - Bang! Headache!

I then pleaded Nosipho to tag along with me to one of the faucets in campus, so that I could drink and splash my face with the only liquid that consisted of only two atoms with similar (not fully) properties but when reacted, form an antagonistic impact - water!

I loved how neutral it tasted and felt when in contact with it - to me it was a sign of normality and calmness - more or less - a feeling of peace and strength would be derived from a splash of water in my face, and a few sips or one gulp would do magic.

Word For The Record: Water is a product of two atoms: Oxygen and Hydrogen. Oxygen is nonflammable, but fire cannot exist in its absence. In fact, we need oxygen to make fire or to keep the fire burning. Interesting, right? Hydrogen is highly flammable. Basically, these two atoms have a positive impact on fire when they are exposed to the fire separately - but when they have reacted (when Hydrogen is burnt into oxygen) to form water - they take down the fire (they have a negative impact on fire). To me - it meant that two are better than one. One person can feed a monster, but two can take it down. Team work is important - even simple elements on a microscopic level know better...

While enjoying the tasteless beverage nature produced without a cost - but entrepreneurs made sure we pay for - Nosipho started with her trailing inability to mind her business by saying, "Mysterious guy *neh*? Seems like the only way to maintain our 'study-partner' relationship is to not poke my nose into your business. What are we eating tonight?"

A thought of 'you still have to go through Bella's proposal' crossed my mind, but because I wanted to dodge that 'visitor', there was no way I would return to my room early. Instead, I asked Nosipho if she didn't mind another session after eating. Having been the nerd that she was, refusing was not optional.

We ate, and when the clock's phalanges subtended seven O'clock post meridiem, I received a call from Toni.

"*Dawg*! Where you at? We gotta rehearse before hitting the stage - and we have only few minutes," Toni said in a worry.

"Flip! I almost forgot... I'm coming up right away, bro - gimme ten."

After hanging up, I apologized to Nosipho for cancelling our pending session and rushed off to my room - but... When I was few metres away from the entrance of KSI, I remembered that I was supposed to avoid meeting up with Sammy. So - I had to apply the T-CUP Rule and I thought of calling Toni. I did and I said, "Dawg, to be honest, I ..."

"Caamaaan - Dawg! You can't disappoint me now!"

"Listen, man - chill - (laughing a little) I actually practiced my piece during the day in campus, so I feel ready, aren't you?"

"That's my *nikka*! I'm always ready - you know! So what do you suggest?"

"Well - we don't really need to rehearse again then... How about you depress now and we'll meet by the entrance of The Orbit?"

"*Ayt* - coming right down - ..."

Before you knew it - we were already at The Orbit, and we performed. He sang an intro´, which became the outro´ as well. When I was reciting my poem, he played a piano in harmony with the tune of the song he sang. However, I was the writer of both the song he sang and the poem I recited.

The title of the poem/song we performed was: *Rus In Vrede, RIP*, (Afrikaans phrase which meant: Rest In Peace), and it went like this...

(Toni)
When they say, "Farewell"
I say, "We'll meet again"
When they focus on saying "bye"
I already see myself, saying "Hi"

So don't trot - don't trot...
Don't trot - I'll catch you on the way...

Don't trot, don't tro-o-o-t - don't trot -
I'll catch you on the waaaaaay...

(MrSir Placidfray)
You don't remember pain,
You just feel it again.
Your mind will only let go
Of what your heart no longer holds.
If it still feels like yesterday,
Then it hasn't gone away.
It's time you put your energy on remedy,
and left all your heartaches at the cemetery.

Rus In Vrede my ouma, my oupa,
Ma en pa, my vriend, my man, my vrou,
My kind en my neef - Rus in Vrede.

If ink was blood,
I'd have empty vessels the way I wrote from the heart.
Finally I'm gonna recite something for you
Without worrying about your level of comprehension
Or your decoding ability.

'Cause you are at a place where language doesn't exist
But messages can be understood.

You are at a place where intellect and struggle are inanimate;

A place where we all wish to go but we aren't as brave
as you were to dare allow a dissociation of our spirit from our flesh.

I'm trying my best to focus on the purpose you served
In this world, rather than the fantasies I had
for the future - with your presence in it.
It's not easy to let go and this is a fact.

I was attached to your presence
More than I was attached to the impact
Your presence brought forth...

I was too fond of your flesh,
More than I was locked onto the purpose you served.

I guess it's true when they say,
"Some lessons in life are best learnt through pain."

I don't wanna dispute God's Will by asking,
"Why you?"
I mean: If not you then who?

But - I still feel like you left us to early.
You've done your part - yes, but
I still haven't had enough of you.

Earth's most precious things weren't in your possession,
But you had the most precious heart that even Bill Gates
Would hesitate to purchase.

You were a character builder -
Not only with your sweet words,
but also by leading as an example.

Your rebuke was loud in meaning
but low in pitch. Mind you?

You taught me the difference between correcting
And shouting...

You were as humble as a child,
but as selfless as a public servant.
Tit for tat might have
Not been applied in response to your kindness,
But you were, without reluctance,
A people's person -
considering our desires before yours.

It's true when they say,
"The Gardener will always pluck off his favorite flower."
I reckoned God loved you more than the way we did and still do.

His Will be done on earth as it is in Heaven.

Rest In Peace my grand mom, my granddad,
Mom and dad, my friend, my husband,
my wife, my child and my cousin.

With these words - I say to everybody here:

You don't remember pain,
You just feel it again.
Your mind will only let go
Of what your heart no longer holds.
If it still feels like yesterday,
Then it hasn't gone away.
It's time you put your energy on remedy,
and left all your heartaches at the cemetery.

Rus In Vrede my ouma, my oupa,
Ma en pa, my vriend, my man, my vrou,
My kind en my neef - Rus in Vrede.
Robala ka kgotso...

(Toni)
When they say, "Farewell"
I say, "We'll meet again"
When they focus on saying "bye"

The Story Of MrSir (Word For The Record)

I already see myself, saying "Hi"

So don't trot - don't trot...
Don't trot, I'll catch you on the way...

Don't trot, don't tro-o-o-t - don't trot -
I'll catch you on the waaaaaay...

"Whooooo! Whooooo!" - Ladies screamed.
"Tjoviiiiitjooo! TjoviiiTjoviiiiii" - Blokes whistled.

Not just applauses and interjections forapproval did us, but also a standing ovation. Yes! They made efforts to fight against gravity, repelling from their warm chairs and their Comfortability -standing for one mission - to approve our performance. Such an effort from strangers was to die for. Through a struggle of unclear images, due to the spotlight that shone bright into my iris, I still managed to see some of the applauders smearing their cheeks with tears - in attempt to wiping them off. While bowing in gratitude to their gratitude and courage-giving, the Master of Ceremony made his way to the stage, touched and teary as well, and started getting deep.

He approached us, looking solemn in the face, and gave us handshakes. After facing the audience, before we could leave the stage, he said, "See? The feeling of losing a loved one is not a mastered feeling, nor is it a feeling you can get used to. You can't even be prepared for it, nor can you be ready for it. When you lose a loved one - the least you can do is accept and let the Supreme Being take charge. Passing away is nothing new in this world; it is just new to each individual in regard to who passes away and how they relate to us. It is an undeniable, unpredictable and inevitable incident that we all have to face, but it doesn't mean it's easy to let go. If you have lost someone in your life - I empathize, be strong *fella*. Ladies and gentlemen - give it up for MrSir Placidfray and Toni!"

Then we left the stage. I was absorbed by the character I wore when I was reciting poetry, feeling the somberness derived from our performance. Just after grabbing a chair to heed the next poet who performed, I wiped the tear that I reluctantly shed, before it could jump off over my lower eyelid. Then I paid attention after the next performer's salutations. Before my phone rang, all I could hear was...

Why is Psychology a difficult Profession to embark on?
Is it because it is the same profession that assisted
colonizers in taking over Africa?
Is it because a nation weak in Psychology is an 'easy to control'
nation?

Why do black people underestimate the impacts of psychological
imbalances?
Why doesn't our education system teach psychology from an early
age?

Medical Doctors will not tell you about the Spiritual Connection sex
has -
They will tell you about using protection for safety.

Pastors will not tell you about the psychological effects of poverty -
They will tell you about how holy it is to not seek earthly things...

See where this is going?

It is said in the old books that,
"Don't ask a Barber if you need a haircut."
Meaning - an advice from a benefitting agent
is not an advice, but a marketing strategy.

Now why would the world introduce Psychology to Africa
But make it a hassle for Africans to professionally acquire
knowledge around it?

The answer is simple: Because it is the world's threat!
If Africans were to be Psychologically strong and understand the
subject
Matter perfectly, we would take our independence and power back!
The reason why Psychology is not Prioritized
Is because the P that stands for Priority in Psychology is silent!

Right now - my hands are shaking from...

Chapter S - Sealing the mystery.

BZZZ! BZZZ! BZZZ!

"Lee! I'm pretty occupied and in a noisy place right now - can I get back to you when I get to my room?"

"Hi - How are you? I'm good, thanks. That's how we answer the phone before updating the caller about our current situations, MrSir! By the way - can't you get to a quiet room? This is urgent."

"Eish - my bad - uhm - *ayt* gimme few sec's..."

Then I swerved across the audience, moving towards the exit door, while the poet's voice was fading due to Doppler Effect. When I was outside The Orbit, I put my phone back to my ear and - we continued...

"Let's talk - what's up?" I asked.

"MrSir - I've received a call from Leticia. She said you didn't wanna talk to her and apparently I'm the closest kin she could get hold of. Can we meet? This is serious."

"Leticia? Why? We have to meet now?"

"Yeah - where are you? I'll collect you and we'll talk over supper, in my flat..."

Word For The Record: Being one with the character on stage, and repelling from that character when you leave the stage is a deep psychological process. In fact - being one with the character of facades in real life, looking alive while dying inside, looking happy when you are sad inside, looking full when your stomach is growling with hunger, and the sundry - is a very deep and dangerous psychological process. We don't really act on stages only, but in our daily lives as well. Psychology should be a lifestyle, not a session.

Indeed, she collected me and we had our 'late' supper at her flat. She prepared a delicious white meal. I considered it 'white' because it had no typical starch items I was used to such as pap, pasta, bread and *'ntonnton'* (what what). However, I enjoyed the food, just not the news...

Out of the blue - she said, "*Mfank'* - I have to commend you on your strength. You are strong, for real. From my professional perspective, people who were targeted like you did are currently in cemeteries, special hospitals or in the streets cleaning our motherland for free. The conversation I had with Leticia didn't uncover everything but in my experience of similar scenarios - my expert assumptions will form a logical conclusion, which will help you with closure..."

"Lee - caamaaan - you not helping in eliminating the anxiety with that long professional speech - let's cut to the chase *hao*. What's really happening here?"

She cleared her throat, and continued, "First - I'm gonna quote Leticia's precise words. Then give you my version of the assumptions. Cool?"

"As long as you gonna say everything there is to be said."

"Leticia - who happens to be your ex - says that the person who Sammy killed is Condolences' brother. Condolences is your ex as well, right?"

"Yeah - but how? Condolences' brother was not an academic, last time I checked. How was he in campus during the time of murder?"

"Let me continue with Leticia's report - she said that Condolences' brother had your camera in his hands at the time of murder, and he was wearing your old clothes. He also had a gun in his possession, which, according to the police research was also meant to kill you."

"Whoa! Wait - my clothes? - And my camera? So this is the culprit? He is the person behind all my losses and confusions? - But how? This doesn't add up! Why was he targeting me? What have I done? - And Sammy? Wasn't he the culprit? This is not real! *Nah* Lee, their report is all a hoax!"

"Mfanak' - lemme finish... Sammy was supposed to be the culprit - he was supposed to be a sacrifice for all this. He also didn't know the whole blueprint until it was almost late. Sammy was supposed to kill you - but what Condolences' brother didn't do was to inform Sammy of his presence during the hit. Basically, Condolences' brother wanted to show you who the real culprit was - which was him - before Sammy could finish his job, then it backfired him."

"- Backfired him? What happened?"

"Since Sammy had known you for years - he knew your clothes as well. So seeing Condolences' brother with your clothes kinda threw him off - that's when everything started taking a turn."

"Wow! This doesn't feel like real life - I feel like I'm watching those American Action Movies!"

"It felt like that when Leticia explained. This case will make her respected in her law field. It's more complicated than we all thought it could be. But this is not all..."

"Yeah - Right! She represents the enemy, mxm!"

"It's her job - loyalty of friendship doesn't pay bills - in fact - she doesn't owe her ex any loyalty, does she?"

"You right, I was selfish to expect anything from her. I'm sorry - to her, of course!"

Then we laughed. In her continuation, she connected the dots...

"This is how Sammy explained the situation at the scene to Leticia, *neh*? He said that when he realized that Condolences' brother had your clothes on, he asked him how he got them. Then Condolences' brother's response made his hackles rise because it was insulting his intelligence. The response was, 'Boy, I don't know what you talking about - *Entlek* (actually) you don't get to ask questions, you do what I paid you to do. When that small boy comes here, you wait for me to say my last words to him and you do the job - okay?'

Then Sammy felt the need to ask about his core intentions, which was when Condolences' brother said, 'Boy Boy Boy! You either shoot the small boy when he comes or I shoot you! What language do I have to use?' Then Sammy lost it when he realized that if he doesn't take that guy down right there, he'll forever live under a boss who doesn't appreciate his loyalty and diligence in being a servant. He remembered that you are the father to his step child and the amount of guilt that hit him instantaneously was enough to end it all. He took it upon himself to just point the gun at Condolences' brother and pulled the trigger without contemplation...

Of course, it was not the first time he killed someone, but it had been a while since he had done it. Now he says that it was definitely the last. He basically saved your life, although he saved it from himself and from his master, Condolences' brother. This is all he knows, all Leticia knows, but - I have my own speculations if you have further questions. Oh - and - before we go any further - if you want psychological sessions, I will recommend an associate of mine - I'll cover the costs. I can't give you sessions during office time when we are this related. Cool?"

"Sure - and thanks for everything so far. I am digesting this and *hai*, it still doesn't add up. I'm just glad I'm alive - I guess coincidence also counts..."

"There you have it, MrSir! Your digressions in your daily activities were impediments to their plots against you. You have to thank the universe for giving you this busy life and so many things to do in a day. According to me - if I connect the dots based on Leticia's report and the stories you shared when we were having lunch - I realized that, you cheated on Leticia with Condolences, although things were a bit cryptic between you and Leticia when you met Condolences, right?"

"Eish - well, I was young and playful - okay - lemme not be euphemistic - I was actually young and stupid! You are right..."

"Perfect! - And you cheated Condolences with Basetsana, right? Basically, after losing Leticia, you continued dating Condolences - then you met Basetsana, right? You started dating her before breaking up with Condolences, right?"

"Mhm! Yeah - where is this going?"

"Then you left Basetsana with a child - although you didn't know... After few years, after playing around without being in any solemn relationship, you met Blessing. Now - Condolences and her 'brother' knew you long before you met them. Do you think it was coincidental? How did his brother mug you - your camera? He followed you from the same pub you met Condolences at, same night. When you returned, you dated his little sister, which became a digression from their initial plan. Their plan was to get the camera from you and bounce - but your charm did the magic..."

"Whoa! Wait - what?"

"For real - Thank whatever you believe in for your looks and 'game', so you call it..."

We laughed - it was adding up but...

"So why did he come for my clothes and laptop?"

"Well, you dated his little sister, changed her, made her a saint, prodded her into leaving the life of theft, then - Boom! You left her for someone else! Remember ya'll - you and Condolences - were supposed to meet the day you met Basetsana, and exactly at Bloed Street. So Condolences saw ya'll and eventually did her own research, reporting to her brother. Why would she? Well - basically, her brother lost a partner in crime, and lost a sister to insanity, 'cause after falling in love for the first time in her life, her psycho tendencies developed. So - according to her brother, you are the cause. So - he was out to get you, to lure you into either giving up on life, so that you could join their criminal crew and substitute his *lil* sister, or to just make you suffer and lose yourself if not to a gunshot. Unfortunately, Sammy didn't play his part 'til the end. Oh – and - as for Basie cheating with Sammy - it was actually supposed to be coincidental as well - but Condolences' brother was the initiator of their rapport."

"It makes sense when you put it like that - but nah - I have to go and sleep on this..."

"Well - MrSir, I am sure. In my experience if these kinda scenarios, this is the only logical assumption. Any other assumption will have many loopholes. I thought about this long and hard before I called you here."

"Let's leave it at that - I'll take that, but I ain't *thunnid* convinced. I'm ninety five percent convinced. It's enough for now... I have to go to my room and sleep, I'm tired, and I don't wanna stress over this - I'm really jubilant over the fact that I'm alive and free from all that psychological drama! My life already feels normal now..."

"What do you usually do when you are emotionally on roller coasters, especially when you are alone?" Lee asked, "However, I'm still shook by your level of emotional intelligence. You - are..."

"I write something..." I replied quickly.

"You never talk to someone - a friend, perhaps?"

"Nah - I just write. My creativity is prodded into activation when I'm emotionally exaggerated - happy, sad, infuriated, - I just feel like writing when I'm not close to my normal moods..."

"Mhm! *Mfanak'* - I think when you get to your room, you'll have to write something. But please - share your writings, either with me or with the whole world. Your experiences can teach us a thing or two about life. *O dibone,* (you've seen it all) *yerrr!*"

When she was taking our plates and cutleries to the dishwashing machine - I already felt like writing a poem. So in my mind, an incomplete piece was formed...

The title of the poem was: *I Want To Write*, and it went like this...

I want to write

I want to write until my fingers become one with the writing instrument,
'Til all the molecules forming the materials of that pen react with my

Fingerprints, and get in some sort of covalent bond...

Oh yes bond - writing is a form of expression that
Allows the boldness of my thoughts to be presented
In fond eyes can perceive and outside world can interpret.
It's a bridge between emotions and expressions, which
Should be crossed with barefoot, 'cause no one should fit
In anyone's shoes when doing the long walk -

I want to write

Because reading can be considered a telepathic
Deliverance of messages since no eye to eye,
Nor simultaneous heed from both sides,
are required, for a thought to reach the audience.

I have to write

Even though I get deep when it spits ink onto the
parchment, as heavy as my thoughts and feelings.
Coloured pens are cherries on top, fillings -
They highlight scenes and ooze films.

So yes, I have to pen down something today -
I have to write - I need to write.

*It gets **Lit** in your mind when you try to **erase***
***Literacy** - for writing is for lighting up retinas of*
Encoders with quantum of mental energy for brain cells
to convert into a prod of a longed activity.
So I have to write - the world needs my writing!

When she returned from doing the dishes, saying "Let's get going - and don't forget to write something tonight, to go back to sanity" ceased my intrapersonal performance half way through and eventually, I considered compiling a poetry journal for publication.

We made our way out of her flat to mine, and when I got into my room - I felt like writing, indeed.

That night, I realized that Psychologists (or just studying psychology for personal gain), are needed in our lives. Just like we ate everyday for energy consumption, went to school every day for knowledge consumption and went to Church every Sunday for spiritual boasting - we also needed to visit psychologists' offices frequently for psychological balances and mental health. That was a need for me, for the culprits themselves and for generations that would come. It was logical to conclude that it was not about losing my items, when they were stolen, but – it was about my mental state. It was a mind control attack!

The poem I wrote when I got into my room, before sleeping, was: *I Just Wonder*, and it went like this...

I thank my mother for not aborting me
when she was pregnant with me.
I also thank my father for not interfering...

The rest of my gratitude goes to
all those who raised me when
My folks chose to not get involved...

Every time when someone tells a story of
How hard their parents worked for them to be
Where they are today, I just wonder, what type
Of kids deserve such parents and why isn't
it all of us? Especially when them parents are
Alive and have good paying jobs - I just wonder!

Is it because we showed them our potential
of doing fine all by ourselves?
Is it a concept of having spoilt folks?
- as progenitors - I just wonder!

If the chromosomes responsible for our complaints
Are shut by our inability to be selfish, or even put
ourselves first for that matter - I just wonder - what
Would happen if we stood up for our right to care,
Charge our genes-donators with negligence, but
Would we ever stop wondering and just do it, well -

I just wonder!

Why would someone enjoy intercourse and
Take to their heels when repercussions show up?
I just wonder...

Indeed - it takes intercourse to make one
A father and a mother -
But it takes responsibility to make them
Mom and dad...

Parents!

Don't invest in your kids
so that you can come back and reap,
when you are not strong anymore...
Invest in them because they carry your genes,
Help them make sure they last long...

See?

When you lose interest in marriage...
When you lose your wallet in a remote place...
When you lose your sight on an exam page...
When you lose your voice on stage...

Those are losses comparable to losing
Your parents' care, love and lives at a young age!

I cheated, I've been cheated on.
I stole, I've been stolen from.
I hurt others, I've been hurt myself.
I did well, I failed as well.
I've been the best, I've been the worst.

I experienced a contradiction of
Characters, personalities and beliefs -
I felt awe, certainties - experienced boredom,
and been involved in fun activities.
I shifted from being egotistic, full of myself,
To being confused, lacking confidence and feeling bad.

I felt like an orphan,
I felt like the only child of my parents.
As much as I was born first,
I still felt like the last.

I sound, look and talk like a spoilt brat,
But reality is I'm on my own and independent!

I'm used to the life of aloneness,
of resilience and self reliance.
No employment, talking about the
right side of cash-flow quadrant.
Perfectionism in high volumes,
but taking it out on school.

Yes - I'm a living paradox,
Mentored by poetic monologue!
My humbleness comes from being looked down on,
My humanity comes from being treated as a pawn,
As for sense of humor, from not being funny at all,
So I would rather have a crooked walk -
than a senseless talk.

I may seem weak, lacking strength and speed,
But damn! I'm blessed with experience and empathy.

It's due to my mysteries and miseries
That I'm for people and my mentees!
I lack energy of acting as someone I'm not,
I have no energy anymore...

When I had energy...

When I had energy, I used it up on being insecure,
That's why I ended up being self employed!

When I had energy I used it up on my trust issues,
I couldn't even trust a tissue - with my tears!
When I had energy I used it up on putting up facades,
The musk is now eliminated by the new musketeer.

The Story Of MrSir (Word For The Record)
Page 174

I shot the fake me, and resurrected as being real!

'Cause I'm tired!

I'm tired of acting cool when I'm hot,
I'm tired of acting full when I can eat the whole pot!

I'm really tired, too tired that I can't
Even run away from the truth...
Too tired that I can't jump into conclusions,
I can't even move with the flow,
I'm sorry ladies, but I'm a tired bloke.

Nicki Minaj was right when she said,
"People will only support you when it's beneficial..."

I'm not complaining, or maybe I am,
But instead of wondering why I'm a mess,
Well - I Just Wonder why I shouldn't be!

Conclusion (T) - Time As An Independent Variable.

"It was all a suicidal mission, MrSir! It was all a mind game. Sammy is actually innocent! He didn't necessarily defend himself - he was manipulated into pulling off the plucks for a coward who wanted to commit suicide. I have just received a call, and they found a note - written by your ex's brother, *Konje* what's her name? Condolences! Yes! Her brother wrote a letter which indicates that he was always aiming at killing himself but he didn't have the balls to do it on his own. You know what, let's meet today for breakfast, and talk this through. The speculations we had were not wrong - but the conclusion was incomplete - this is really an awesome case, (coughs) sorry for sounding insensitive! You might be free MrSir. You might be psychologically at ease!"

Lee called me at exactly 3A.M, when I was quarter way through having an average healthy sleep. She didn't even greet, neither did she try to prepare my mind to shift from dreaming to being awake for a full comprehensive capacity for her complex ´case breakthrough.´

Did I sound relieved? Did I even understand any of her hunches and and and...? Well - I heard, but I did not listen. I just replied with, "Wow! I'm free? Let's talk during breakfast, thanks Lee!"

She was a Psychologist - of course - she knew that I did not pay heed. So she just said, "Breakfast it is - I'll explain again, don't worry. Go back to your shuteye, *Mfank'* - stay well..."

Then I hung up.

Instead of reminiscing over the words she said, I just felt like easing the tension by calling my girlfriend. There was something about midnight thoughts and feelings that I couldn't fully understand - they were focal and severe. Any of those moments were like that.

Which explained why stressing and straining thoughts deprive people of their sleeps around those times, their brains somehow were on their focal and severe activeness. I thought it was because all parts of our bodies were relaxing and disturbances of daily duties, social activities and the sundry were not our concerns, and part of me knew that I would always think that. However, it wasn't just stressing and straining thoughts that would be focused and severe, relaxing and romantic thoughts too. When the clock approached midnight from either sides, conversations would get 'adult conceptual' if not just deep. Countryside people of South Africa would tell you that midnight was also time for praying if not for witches or wizards - deep stuff. Studying around midnight every night could guarantee you a B. Midnight was a perfect time for depth, you reckon!

The reason why I called my girlfriend was simply because she was my niche! She was my mental comfort zone - deep mental relaxation episodes of my life had been in her control since I started dating her - where I would care less to nothing about the world and its complexities. She was like a plateau at the crest of Table Mountain, where I recharged emotional strength to face the slope of life's downward steepness.

"Baybe, wake up and sip rooibos tea," I said, right after she had picked up, before she could greet.

"Mhmmm! Morning love, what time is it?"

"It's around 3 - I miss you."

"I miss you more - but, why so early?"

It kind of set me off when she said that she missed me more. She was half awake and could barely feel different to anything she perceived. So - saying that she missed me more after I said that I missed her was just a subconscious response almost every couple felt the need and obligation to cite when their partners expressed their 'missing' feelings. It was not necessary, but it explained why 'lying to make someone feel special' existed in the first place. It was not harmful to lie like that, 'cause she was highly unlikely to be in control.

However, I noticed that she did not say that because that was how she felt - she said it because I said it. It was a funny subtle observation that would later instigate few concepts of how our minds work. That was an observation I made because I had just spoken with Lee - so she kind of reeled my focus to how our minds work.

From then on, attention to detail became my second nature, and I slowly and lightly made sense of the call I had with Lee. I guess I was getting awake myself too...

"I wanted to talk to the only person who mattered equally to my daughter, and - guess what - it's you. Your voice is seductive around this time - why am I not with you?" I said.

She giggled a little and replied with, "Don't get in the mood in my absence - why so early though? Were you serving THEE internet?"

She emphasized 'THEE' to hint me on the type of scenes she was implying that I was watching - and, that on its own made me reminisce over our first date! I started missing her more than I did when I told her that I did.

"Nah baybe, caamaaan... But on that note, I'll try not to get in the mood without you. I called you because I wanted to shift my focus from yesterday's tragedies - since you the only person who seem to have all it takes to substitute Headache Tablets. Something happened and it doesn't make complete sense. I will explain today in the afternoon, 'cause this call is specifically about us talking about us - not about stressful incidents, mind you?"

"You are the man! But, *word for the record* - I don't mind talking about anything you wanna talk about, and at any given time of the day. Don't ever forget that."

"I appreciate it, my love - I appreciate you. To what do I owe the pleasure of having you in my life though?"

"To the pleasure of having you in mine," Before I could respond - she continued, "Babe, can I sleep - I have a long day today. I need all the rest I could get. You'll be alright, right?"

"Yeah! Sure. Just hearing your voice was therapeutic. Imagining you was meditative, and..."

"Woah! Love, if you start, you won't finish. You and your eager to win me even when you are at the finishing line though - will you ever claim your trophy?"

"I doubt! Thing is, Sweetness, you are not a goal, you are a process. I'll love you collaboratively with showing you consistently. You are more like a..."

"Goodnight *Munchie*, don't be too much in the mood *neh*? I love you."

Then I laughed and threw in the towel, "Goodnight my *Love'cado*. Be beautiful..."

To be honest, I wanted to keep the conversation as long as possible. Even though we didn't necessarily have a productive discussion of anything considered significant in life, I still felt like each conversation we had was the best I had in that particular time. My heart was getting more and more familiar with being fond of her - and love was getting validated by my mind. In simple terms, I was falling for her...

After hanging up I reeled my focus back to the conversation I had with Lee - talking about a sleepless night!

Before the clock could strike four ante meridiem, when I comprehended what Lee said, I realized that Depression is deeper than how I thought. I was getting scared of being the victim of it, and also being the cause of it in other people's lives. I wondered why it took me that long to even realize that then. I considered taking Lee's advice on consulting with a Psychologist, but my best internal therapy session was writing - so I took Poetry Journal Of MrSir *(Views & Emotions)* and wrote a poem on depression. That poem helped me understand and empathize with the culprit (Condolences' brother) but, it also made me wonder how strong his depression was for him to be so focused on his mission. I started wondering how he grew up, why he did the things he did, etc - basically everything that led him to mental breakdown. I told myself that I would seek understanding before judging, from then on...

The title of the poem was: *Time You Took Me Serious!* And it went like this...

*Hello, I am **Adrenalin**!*
*Some call me **Strength**.*
*Even though we all know that I'm just **Impulse**.*
*I'm the only child of **Anxiety** and **Fear** -*
*Closest cousin to **Nervousness**, **Pain**, and the sundry*

*My Scientific stage name is **Reflex Arc**!*
*But - my biggest fans call me **Anger** -*
*Yet the naive still call me **Nothing Serious**...(huh)*

I guess I'm based on who you want me to be -

*See I'm all about **psychology** -*
Complex like mathematics, deeper than history -

Irrational like religion and rational than philosophy.
I'm in dual properties like light -
But I'm the absence of it - I'm darkness!

I'm the reason ropes are lacing on necks
With no intention for swag!
Yeah - the elephant in the room...
No one dares to make me a topic when dining,
Especially in black neighborhoods.

It's funny 'cause everyone knows that I exist,
Since I cause and result in divorces and abuses -
I'm in dual properties!

*Care to know what they call me in **diagnostic terms**?*
Take a wild guess...

I build up on architectures of childhood grudges
Roofed by cyber bullies and social injustice.
When you supposed to figure me out with your knees on Tiles, praying,
You allow me to pave the way that leads
You directly to extreme alcohol consumption!

See? I'm tricky - I'm the enemy within you
That you choose to ignore -
Because you are very talented in letting things slide
Until the last minute -
Until you face death -
I'm that evil, it's time you took me serious!

Yeah - I can have my ways with your subconscious reactions -
*My kingdom is called **Amygdala** -*
Which means - you have little to no control over me,
Once I get into you - you become me,
And I become me -

See? There's no space for your ruling,
Since I don't give you time to heed your neocortex,
I delegate your nervous system with my evil plans,
I'm fast and powerful -
It's time you took me serious!

You can only defeat me with what matters more than IQ -
Not money - to eradicate me you have to first accept that I'm part of
you -
But because you are too egotistic and righteous,
You usually take too long to let your guts down,
And the durations you take give me enough time
To bulk up and even get to extents of affecting your life as a whole -
Until it's late to alleviate damages...
It's really about time you took me serious!

Sometimes I'm accepted into your lives
Through what you mistake with motivations -
Like when you use comparison to motivate your children,
That's pretty much of a door for me to budge in -
Instead of them doing good to compete,
They seek adoption from my parents:

*A little reminder - **Anxiety and Fear** -*

Of failure, in activities that aren't even aligned with their purposes
Because instead of taking time to study your child's abilities
You would rather pressurize them into doing what you failed to do.
So, one of my niches is where parents force children to live their
dreams.

Sometimes you mistake my victims with culprits
When, really, their deeds are just my side effects -

Like: handcuffing a rapist, a child molester
Or a woman abuser -

The Story Of MrSir (Word For The Record)

Instead of rehabilitating him -
In this case,
I attack a man and as a side effect -
He becomes a criminal,
So instead of diagnosing him with me,
And provide the right help -
You choose to punish him with imprisonment
For acting upon my side effect -

Bear with me -
I'm not saying that immoralities and criminal activities,
Don't require justice to be done -
I'm not saying that the bad can't have control over me!

They can - but through a priority...

I'm just saying - I am the cause of badness in most instances,
So the moment I'm given enough attention,
The moment you accept me and treat me,
Police officers will run out of jobs,
'cause a lot of jails would be empty!
It's time you took me serious!

I'm not really after being on hash tags,
With no sincerity and genuineness,
With no willingness to act
Upon dealing with me - I'm your enemy,
But you are my meal - I feed off you.
Don't just make me trend - but
Take me serious!

You want to know what I fear?

Mental health!

If you prioritize it, I'll play magic on you -

I'll disappear for good...

*I am **Real** -*
Let me reintroduce myself,
*My name is **Depression**!*
It's time you took me serious!

My mental energy was drained for centuries! Having written two poems in one 'moon time interval' was not *pap en vleis* (an Afrikaans version of 'open and shut case'). At around half past six ante meridiem I was already through with *Time You Took Me Serious*, so I decided to check up on Condolences - not a good idea!

Condolences was my ex - for anything sake! Our 'first date memory' was a Sci-Fi movie scene - quite futuristic! However, our last conversation was a horror movie scene - if we had an audience they would not have me as part of them. Regardless of the given condition, the irrational part of my brain made me search for her number and I called her. Not because I wanted to send my condolences to her, for the loss of her brother, but because I wanted to dig more background on them - both of them, actually. I wanted to understand how her brother turned out to be the way he was, why he did the things he did, and to also understand why they were criminals to begin with. I needed answers, not realizing that I was not necessarily simplifying my life, I was complicating it further. I thought everything had answers and some logical explanations. I thought all things should have definite meaning or at least comprehension. I believed in closure.

Word For The Record: No molecules and compounds have no spaces in between after reaction. Our skins have pores, wrappers have microscopic pores... Everything has pores, but the sizes differ. What penetrates through one material may not pass through another. In Chemistry, the concept of 'definite closure' does not exist. Even in life - there's always a loophole. What was definite in

*one era creates a loophole in another. Closure is relative to Time -
it is rather a variable than a fixed point.*

"Hello," she answered.

"Hi, uhm - it's MrSir *neh*? How are you?"

"I'm - good, thanks and how are you?" Her tone was composed and
it sounded like a contemplating thought processed when you
answered multiple choice questions without having a clue of which
one was the right option among all the options given.

I was sort of speechless, but I tried to keep up, "I'm getting there.
My condolences, hey..."

"I'm yours now? Are you okay?"

"You are mine? I'm lost..."

"Didn't you just say your Condolences?"

"Oh! Nah! Not in reference to your name - my bad. I'm referring to
your brother."

"What about my brother? MrSir - stop beating about the bush and
out with it!"

"I thought you already heard - I'm sorry to be the bearer of the
news... Your brother passed on..."

After going 'out with it' with the sad news, she became silent for
almost seven seconds. Just when I was about to check if it was bad
reception disconnecting us, I heard a sound of her heavy breath
accompanied by her effort of pulling back mucus up her nostrils. It
sounded as though she was trying hard not to cry out loud but she
was really hurt, I could sense. I did not know what to do, and in so

being blank towards the predicament, I immediately sidelined my initial aim for the call. I ceased wanting to dig on his brother's intentions with my life and attempted to be a shoulder to cry on.

I said, "I'm really sorry about what happened - and I know I wasn't his favorite person but, I empathize with you right now. If you need anything, hala back. Be well, and see a psychologist."

"What happened? How did you know? Is this really true?"

"He got shot - I don't know thorough details of the incident but the person who shot him, apparently, was his colleague of some sort. I think..."

"He better hide forever, 'cause if not - we are coming for him! Not with my brother! Not with him!"

"Whoa! Condolences - please promise me one thing – promise me that you'll see a psychologist before the funeral and after, please? They are available at no cost in government hospitals. Then we'll talk afterwards. I'm also here if you need me."

"For real, MrSir - I'm coming for him! I'll see the psychologist, send me more details about the one you recommend most. But as for the person who killed my brother? I'm definitely coming for his back!"

"Be well, Condolences - be well..."

Then I hang up before she replied. I couldn't take it. I had a lot in my plate already, and I couldn't add Condolences' bargain to my meal. I just couldn't. All I wanted was to understand why his brother came after me so hard - and so persistently - not to be his little sister's shoulder to cry on. I needed a shoulder to cry on - how could I have been one when I needed one myself? How could life be that unfair? I complained in my heart until the sun appeared. That was it - that time interval of seeing a new sunny day was a turn of events for me. I finally understood what to balance one's life meant. Time was indeed an independent variable! What we made of it was dependent on our mindsets and perceptions. I chose to empathize with her rather than judging her - but, I also chose to let go.

Having realized that Lee's explanation would have still been a speculation, I considered not heeding it anymore. I only took the explanation where she referred to taking depression serious - indeed it was real. Therefore, I just considered what she urged me with: Seeing a psychologist. From then on - I was also going to suggest it to everyone who went through something. The same way we used to recommend pastors for spiritual problems, medical doctors for medical problems, teachers or facilitators for educational problems - I learnt that, as much as we were human in flesh and spirit - we were also human in our minds, and what better way could one be well fully without taking care of their minds?

About The Author

Mpho Matlhabegoane is a young South African adult, aged 25 (at the time of publishing), who was born in a village called Taung, North West (mother land) - and he was moved in the absence of his parents to another (developing) village called Mmametlhake, Mpumalanga (father land) at the age of four.

After teaching Mathematics as a private teacher during his gap year between his matriculation and tertiary first year study - his skills and knowledge were broaden from one sector to another...

He is a Mathematics Facilitator, Financial Literacy Facilitator, Emotional Intelligence Facilitator, Motivational Speaker, Service Philanthropist, Poet, Writer, Entrepreneur, Career Coach and (not limited to) Mentor to young leaders.

He embarked on the journey of writing due to his interesting life experience which he published a nonfiction short essay about, memoir, titled: Why I Write Books. He taught mathematics in different schools and gave motivational talks in different departments including Dept of Education, Dept of Health and others. As a product of reading a lot, he became a self made fiction writer. He worked for Brain Waves Development Organization as an All Rounder and Mentor under the mentorship of the Founder and CEO. He also worked for Uhunu Career Guidance and Learning (Pty) Ltd as a manager.

He is a Founder and Director of Mr Sirs Potential Target (Pty) Ltd, which is a self publishing and book distribution company that also provide with services not limited to extra classes and private tutorials of challenging subject contents for FET Learners (including high schools). Ultimately, he is a simplifier - and this book is about simplifying life...

Dedication and Acknowledgement

*As late as I may be, this story is dedicated to my late
mother, Elsie Tuabeng, who left our world at least
three months prior to the release date of this book.
She was a victim of psychological attack for all my
life and never had the privilege of receiving
professional help from those who understood her
state. Subtly and solemnly, she is the reason why I am
embarking on literature journey and the reason why
I'm investing my energy on spreading awareness of
the seriousness of mental health – her legacy is
instilled in my style of story-telling, type of writing
and intellect. Long live, your spirit of inspiration,
long live!*

My acknowledgement goes to all my associates,
known as First Stack Buyers: *MSPT Mentees*,
Activators and the organization at large, distributors,
family – my father (Jerry Matlhabegoane) and closest
cousin (Abram Morokana Matlhabegoane), my initial
publisher and compilation advisor; Tebogo
Hlongwane, friends and loyal fans, I say, thank you
for your support, valuable contribution and
inspirations.
Special gratitude to all those who proofread my work
and contributed in additions of relevant concepts
before the final piece could go public: Katlego
Seshoka, Boitshoko Bokaba (*Poetic B*), Buyisiwe
Mazibuko, Kelebogile Tompa, Resaoleboga
Leutlwetse, Mmagauta Mokoena (*Tricy Gee*) and
Tsholofelo Mokoena.
Some of them (associates) weren't even readers, but
still made efforts to purchase this copy and read it.
Final thanks to everyone who laid a hand on this book
- I hope you learnt and enjoyed the contents. Reading
this book is *The Beginning of Mental Evolution*!

www.ingramcontent.com/pod-product-compliance
Lightning Source LLC
Chambersburg PA
CBHW051513170626
46811CB00002B/792